FIX

FIX

J. ALBERT MANN

LITTLE, BROWN AND COMPANY
New York   Boston

Copyright © 2021 by Jennifer Mann

Cover silhouette by Neil Swaab. Cover pill art © mecaleha/istockphoto.com. Cover hand-lettering and design by Karina Granda. Cover copyright © 2021 by Hachette Book Group, Inc.

Little, Brown and Company
Hachette Book Group
1290 Avenue of the Americas, New York, NY 10104
Visit us at LBYR.com

First Edition: May 2021

Little, Brown and Company is a division of Hachette Book Group, Inc. The Little, Brown name and logo are trademarks of Hachette Book Group, Inc.

The publisher is not responsible for websites (or their content) that are not owned by the publisher.

Library of Congress Cataloging-in-Publication Data
Names: Mann, J. Albert, author.
Title: Fix / J. Albert Mann.
Description: First edition. | New York : Little, Brown and Company, 2021. | Audience: Ages 14+. | Summary: In the aftermath of major surgery, sixteen-year-old Eve struggles with pain, grief, and guilt while becoming increasingly dependent on pain medication, revisiting memories of her best friend, and exploring a potential romance.
Identifiers: LCCN 2020048433 | ISBN 9780316493499 (hardcover) | ISBN 9780316493406 (ebook) | ISBN 9780316493437 (ebook other)
Subjects: CYAC: Surgery—Fiction. | Scoliosis—Fiction. | Best friends—Fiction. | Friendship—Fiction. | Drug addiction—Fiction. | Mothers and daughters—Fiction.
Classification: LCC PZ7.1.M36614 Fix 2021 | DDC [Fic]—dc23
LC record available at https://lccn.loc.gov/2020048433

ISBNs: 978-0-316-49349-9 (hardcover), 978-0-316-49340-6 (ebook)

Printed in the United States of America

LSC-C

Printing 1, 2021

For Kevin Mann

The only lie I've ever told my children
is that we make our own lives.
You made my life.

Nineteen Degrees

I'M COLD.

―――――

Cold and confused.

―――――

Do I feel the tube between my lips? The staples sunk deep into my torso? The bars and screws bolted to my spine? The pain?

―――――

No. All I feel is cold.

―――――

A warm shadow lingers over me. I hear her. Maybe. Then... nothing.

I dream of soft blurry voices and distant bright lights. Slowly, so slowly, I realize these aren't dreams at all, but reality flittering into focus.

Colors.

Sounds.

Everything hazy and high-pitched and filled with beeping and clicking and the whooshing sounds of air.

At some point, they pull the tube from my throat. I think about screaming but then forget.

Nearby, I hear someone calling out over and over. I beg them to *please* stop—although only in my head—because my voice is off somewhere. Lost.

I see the light of day coming in through a window. And I hear Dr. Sowah, talking, laughing. *Where is my mother?*

"Eve!"

Someone calls to me from a distance, as if I'm floating far away from them.

"'Ey, lazy, open up those eyes. You can totally 'ear me." It's Dr. Sowah. His missing *h* so familiar. He always joked that he left that letter back in Ghana when he came over at age eighteen.

I think I must have smiled because he chuckles. Dr. Sowah is always chuckling.

"That's right, I know you're there."

Am I? Or am I on a river?

Sliding along in the sunshine.

Safe.

Warm.

Happy.

Until he leans over me, blocking out the sun like a rain cloud. "Eve, I'm delighted to report that you are officially nineteen degrees."

Nineteen degrees?

It's easy to hear his pride in that number.

Nineteen.

But I can't wrap my head around it.... This new Cobb angle measuring the tilty twist of my spine. Large progressive scoliosis meant my forever-collapsing spine was forever producing a new one. Forty-eight degrees...fifty-two... sixty-seven...who could keep track? Although, this one— nineteen—is now fixed to me.

By titanium.

The river spins me. Then stops flowing with a loud snap, sending a searing shudder all along that nineteen-degree angle.

The beginning of the second week in Massachusetts General Hospital is filled with pain, needles, thirst, and screaming— mostly mine.

I am pinned under cold wet skin and bones. I can't breathe from the terrifying pain, the fear that this bloodied slab is forever on me, in me, is me.

Then . . . there is the shuffle near my IV. The surge of air deeply entering my lungs. And me, grasping at the nearest scrubs—to let them know they saved me, they have to keep saving me—before I'm floating off again on that river, light as a duck feather.

———

Sometimes I wake up screaming in the light.

———

Sometimes I wake up screaming in the dark.

———

Every time I open my eyes, and even when I don't, I scramble for the button to my morphine pump and cry out to Martin, the nice nurse, regardless if it's his shift. And there he is, bending over my arm with an extra dose.

A rush of saliva.

A sting.

And I hear her again.

———

"Martin," I whisper. "She's here. Lidia."

"It's the drugs, baby," Martin tells me. "No one's here."

Red Rover,
Red Rover

When I was six years old, I could
not imagine being anything but
strong and fast and tough.

I thought as much about my spine
twisting deep inside me
as I did about the world's economy
or my mother's day at work—which meant
not at all.

I wanted to play.
I always wanted to play.
And couldn't believe my luck
that sunny afternoon
when a game of red rover
began around me.

Hand slapped into
hand slapped into
hand. Forming

a human chain. A chain
I wasn't part of.

Turning every which
way, desperate
for entry—there she stood
reaching out with an arm
that did not end
in a hand.

Not knowing what to do
I did nothing.
But she knew.

"Take it,"
she said.

I took it.
Clutching the arm where it ended,
a little way up from where a wrist
would be.

Our line began to chant.
Red rover, red rover,
send Justin over.

Across the field,
a kid in stiff new jeans

and a Red Sox T-shirt
broke from the line
and started running toward us.
Fast.
Toward us.
Me and the girl.
Me and Lidia.

"Hold on," she screamed.

And I did.

Please, No

"Hold on, darlin', I'm about to remove your catheter," Martin says. "It's time to get out of that bed."

I don't bother opening my eyes.

"You're gonna have to move sooner or later, little Evie."

I feel a dry sting from deep behind my belly button all the way down to my knees.

The sting fades.

I fade with it.

I'm never moving.

———

But they come.

The physical terrorists.

———

Talking. Touching. Positioning.

Please. Please, no. It hurts. Please.

Moving my blankets, my gown, my limbs.

No. Please, no. I can't. Stop.

⟶

They don't stop. They sit my body up. And then they stand it up. While I scream so loud the sound comes out my eye sockets.

It's like someone has stuck a metal rod straight up my ass, through my torso, and into my shoulder blades. Because they have.

As I choke on a thick mix of sweat and tears and snot, my head rolls about at the end of my neck, giving me a swirling view of ceiling, floor, curtains. The PTs mutter "Shhh" and "It's okay," standing on either side of me, holding me upright. Not that it's a hard job—I haven't eaten anything for almost two weeks and I'm pretty sure my hospital gown weighs more than I do.

My utter lack of compliance does nothing to convince them to return me to my bed so I try begging—saying the word *please* so many times it's really just my lips quivering with fear.

They continue like they can't hear me. The short woman saying "You can do this," and the taller repeating "Yes, you can do this," in an even louder voice over and over. It's like I'm trapped in some strange torturous pep-talk echo chamber, and I can't tell if these two are physical therapists or personal trainers.

Together, they drag me across the hospital room while I sob, and the old lady I share the room with shouts, "Jesus H. Christ, take me," and "Holy Mother of God, shut her up," in a cigarette-induced Southie rasp.

It isn't even a ten-foot journey, but every muscle I need to take those steps has been sawed through and then stapled back together.

My mother walks in. Her face drops, and she quickly backs out the door. "I'll come back when you're done."

What? No. Help!

But she's gone.

The PTs cart me into the bathroom, position my hands on the bars on either side of the toilet, and hike up my gown. Immediately, I remove my hands to clutch at them, pleading through my tears for someone to do something to stop the pain.

Again they reposition my hands and attempt to lower me to the pot, but my gown falls down first. Up I come as they attempt to tie the gown out of my way.

"Just take the goddamn thing off," I snap.

The tall PT gently removes my gown, and together, they lower my body onto the toilet, resting each of my arms on one of the bars. I beg them not to leave me like this. I can't do it. I can't stay here. It hurts too much. Everything hurts too much.

Staying true to their infuriating optimism, they leave

me and pull the door closed half an inch—like I need privacy after having just been placed naked onto a toilet.

I cling to the bars, my head dangling from my neck, my rib cage and spine on fire. I've stopped crying, and the lingering panting and hiccups send shocks of pain from my knees to my eyes.

I sit.

And sit.

Nothing happens. It's like the pee doesn't know how to come out of me without a tube.

My physical therapy cheerleading squad keeps up their chanting outside the bathroom, which does nothing to help. Finally, the short PT comes back in and turns on the faucet. As she exits, she pulls the door almost completely closed, and I'm left staring at my reflection in a full-length mirror.

There was a time—called my entire fucking life—when I'd have done anything to see myself in a mirror with a Cobb angle of nineteen degrees, but now all I see are staples.

Large staples.

Large, metal staples.

Many, many large, metal staples. A gleaming railroad track sunk deep into my pale white skin and crisscrossing a thick red slice of open wound traveling from under my armpit, down past my belly button, and around my hip.

What did they do to me? What did they do?

Forgetting I can't, I jump up and then fall back onto the toilet, hitting the seat hard. The pain is so horrible that I can do nothing but cling to the bars while blood pounds in my temples.

One of the PTs calls my name.

I can't answer. I'm sliding. Sliding from the toilet. Sliding toward the floor, where my staples will catch on the seat and rip me open. I'm going to be ripped open and I'm going to hurt worse than I do right now.

Fear overwhelms me. And just as my sweaty hands slip from the bar, the PTs rush into the room and grab my arms, righting me.

Nineteen degrees? Who the hell cares.

I'm shouting. Or screeching. My voice needing to mimic the pain.

The PTs try to calm me down as they shove my arms back into my gown. I won't be calmed. *That wasn't me.* How could anyone live looking like this?

The old lady howls profanity while the PTs haul me past her toward my bed. I'm sobbing and hyperventilating at the same time. Every breath yanking mercilessly at my staples.

Martin, the nice nurse, is behind me. He has a needle in his hand. My needle.

When they roll me onto my bed, it feels like someone is ripping my spine right out through my neck. Martin sticks me even as I scream into his face.

I keep on screaming until the morphine turns my screams into hoarse moans, and then finally into nothing at all.

"Martin," I gasp. "I didn't pee."

"Yes, you did, sweet baby." He laughs. "I'm gonna go clean it up off the bathroom floor right now."

"Martin," I say, clutching him. My throat burns. Somehow, he knows, and he shovels in a spoonful of ice chips.

Holy Mother of God, that feels good.

God

The first time I
officially heard His name
was in school.
The Pledge of Allegiance.

Although I'd certainly
seen churches—for me
they were curious buildings with doors
I'd never walked through.

In this pledge,
which I was asked
to repeat each morning, we were
under Him.

I didn't get it, so
I asked my mother.

"God doesn't like women,"
she said.

In my mother's defense,
I probably asked while

she was in the middle of grading undergraduate papers
or
composing feminist verse
and I'm sure she didn't consider
for a second
I'd take her statement
and think about it
for as long as I did.

God didn't like me much.
The weird thing was,
I felt Him
not liking me.

I was diagnosed with scoliosis at eight.
By twelve, my spine was twisting
into the squirrely shape
of a loopy S.

A band of muscles
was beginning to collect
on my back.

It wasn't a hump
yet.

My shoulder blade
hadn't protruded—

awkwardly stretching my skin tight
in one place
while folding it into elephant-like wrinkles
in another. My rib cage
didn't scrape my hip. And
my life of being
photographed from behind,
faceless,
had not begun.
But it was coming.
It was all coming.
And I wanted it to stop.

One evening my mother caught me
in front of my bedroom mirror
standing in my underwear and
holding myself in such a way
that I might look
straight.

Ashamed,
I tried to explain.

"That imperfect reflection,"
she said, "is
all in your head."

Was it?
This imperfection.
All in my head?

Of course
I thought about Lidia.

Was Lidia's
missing hand
all in her head?

But Lidia was missing something.
That was real.
I wasn't missing anything.
I had a spine.

Two facts Dr. Sowah
gave me when I was eight:
    1. In most cases of scoliosis
            there is no known cause,
                 and
    2. In all cases,
            there is no cure.

This second part brought me back to
God.

I prayed.

Lidia prayed,
too.

For my spine.
Not her hand.
Spines having
nothing to do
with hands,
back then.

By the time I turned thirteen,
I prayed only that He stop
the twisting.

Lidia prayed
harder.
And I thought,
Who wouldn't listen
to Lidia?
I always listened
to Lidia.

He didn't.

By fourteen, I was begging for a miracle.
Lidia begged, too.

For my spine and
for her hand.
Spines and hands being equal
when it came to miracles, and
breasts and hips beginning to make miracles
more necessary.

By fifteen Lidia said,
"God can
fuck himself."
I couldn't help feeling
fucked, too.

I once read that females are eight times more likely than
males to progress to a curve magnitude requiring
        treatment.

Maybe my mother was right.

The Telescope

THE FIRST THING I SEE WHEN I OPEN MY EYES IS THE STREET-light shining through my bedroom window. The second is my mother. She's holding a glass of water and saying something about running to the office for a couple of hours. She won't be long.

The office?

She slides my phone closer to me on my bedside table while she talks about her staggering workload.

She's going to work?

How it's been piling up because of all the time she spent in the hospital.

She's leaving me?

But it's only my second night home. I'll be alone. Though not totally alone. My mind drifts to the box under my bed. But then my mother picks up my orange bottle and my heart jumps along with the Roxanol tablets as she removes the cap and hands me a smooth pill.

So light.

Sticking it in my mouth, I sip from the straw my mother holds to my lips and swallow, already caring less about boxes or being alone. The chalky Roxy sticks in my throat for a second, making my eyes tear up. She lowers my shade—halfway, due to her hurry—and I watch her go through a weepy blur.

I listen to her bumping about, getting ready to leave.

The apartment door closes.

A few moments later there is the rumble of a car motor. The crunch of gears. And then her engine fading away.

How long did she say she'd be gone?

I glance over at my phone. It sits next to a bell my mother placed there yesterday so I can ring it if I need her. How many things do I need to call someone who isn't there?

Reaching out, I pick up my phone, squinting at its bright blue light.

Hitting Messages, I stare at her picture and name sitting second from the top. It's not at the top because Thomas Aquinas is at the top. Again.

I delete his text.

Again.

I should put my phone down, but my thumb hovers for just a second . . . and then I'm doing it. Typing her name.

Lidia.

And swooshing it out into the universe.

Staring at the screen, I'm not really waiting. I know what will happen. Nothing. Nothing will happen.

Nothing happens.

Not being able to stand the stillness of it, I press call and listen to it ring. Listen to the mailbox-is-full message.

I call again.

This time, the ringing seems to go on forever. When I hear the click of the robot voice as it comes back on to tell me what I already know, I snap the phone off, not wanting to hear its soullessness.

Instead, I listen to the throbbing of blood in my ears.

I sigh. Just to hear a bit of noise.

It's not enough.

"Hello," I say, to no one. To myself… maybe.

Minutes pass. And like butter melting into a warm piece of toast, the Roxy begins to soak through the millions of cell walls throughout my body. The scratchy flutter in my chest settles, but the pain never fully, truly leaves. It's like a shark circling me in dark water.

I don't mind that the pain stays nearby. I actually kind of like it. It reminds me how lucky I am to *know* I'm no longer in pain. If the Roxanol erased everything, I probably wouldn't appreciate the pills half as much as I do.

Now I lie listening to the nothingness. Unlike the hospital, home is silent. And dark. My toes slide into a cooler spot under my covers while my eyes wander about the room. They stop on my telescope.

It's not really *my* telescope. It's my mother's. Although I don't think she's ever used it. She bought it in one of her fits of feeling like she needed to expand herself—the same way she ended up with the jumble of mountain-climbing equipment still in its packaging in the storage space, or the barely worn martial arts uniform folded neatly on her closet shelf. Or the way she decided to be artificially inseminated to have me.

I rescued the telescope from the hall closet, thinking I'd use it one day. And I do use it. Kind of. To hang clothes on that aren't dirty enough to throw into the hamper but aren't clean enough to hang back up.

There are no clothes thrown over it tonight, and the light from the streetlamp makes the black cylinder glow. I stare at the sheen. Slowly, the telescope bends and twists, stretches and turns. And when it speaks to me, I'm not surprised or scared.

"How do you do, Miss Abbott?"

I grin at the extreme formality. It seems like how a teapot should sound, not a telescope.

I'm also not surprised it knows my name. Lots of things know me. Roxanol makes the world come alive with movement, and everything and anything can become animate. In the hospital, the people on my little TV spoke to me all the time. And last night, on my first night home, the stuffed rabbit Lidia gave me for my tenth birthday woke me from a sound sleep and accused me of stealing its house keys. I didn't steal them, and I didn't know what to do. So I called

Lidia. It was the millionth time I'd called her since that night, though the first time I'd done it at four o'clock in the morning. I knew she wouldn't pick up. Maybe that's why I called again. And then twenty or so more times after that... whispering a bunch of stuff that I don't remember following the beep. I do remember that once I filled her voice mail, I called her mother next. Why, I don't know. It was four o'clock in the morning, and you always do weird shit at four o'clock in the morning.

Mrs. Banks answered. I wish I hadn't cried so much. But she was as kind as ever. In her soft Polish accent, she told me to go back to sleep and said that she was sure I'd find the rabbit's house keys tomorrow. For a minute, it felt just like the old days when Lidia took care of everything. I hung up and fell asleep, hoping that just like the old days, Lidia would show up in the morning.

She didn't.

"Miss Abbott?" The telescope persists.

I glance over at the bell. Would my mother hear it ringing from her office at the community college? Maybe she didn't really go to work. Maybe she went out with Mary Fay. My mother likes Mary Fay a lot. I know because she's been dating her for four years, and my mother has never dated anyone that long. Does my mother like me a lot? I have this urge to ring the bell. But I'm afraid she won't come.

"How are you tonight, Miss Abbott?" Its voice seems to be rising from deep within the long cylinder leading to the lens.

"Not that good," I answer.

There's no reason to lie to my telescope.

I see myself reflected in the dark circle of the lens, which is facing me instead of the stars. My nose looks very large and wide, and my long hair is wild on one side and smashed flat on the other. I always wanted a short bob, but Lidia insisted it looked better long.

"Let me help," the telescope says. "Have you ever been to Minnesota?" it asks.

I sigh. "You mean the state shaped like a mitten?"

"That's Michigan," it says.

Being corrected by my telescope makes me feel like the sun is setting inside my chest.

"I feel like shit," I confess. "Just so . . . so shitty."

My body fills with a tremendous ache that rolls and swells and heaves itself against my sawed-off ribs, my tender spine, my fresh incisions lined with staples.

"I can help," says the telescope, the sound of his deep voice making the hairs on the back of my neck come alive and the terrible aching recede.

"How?" I sniff.

"Leave the how to me. Just tell me something: Have you ever been to Minnesota?"

Minnesota? "Please, I'm so tired . . ."

"Eve."

He uses my first name. The sound of it wrapping warmly around me.

"No," I tell him.

"Do you care about Minnesota?" he asks quietly.

Cold. Lakes. Snow.

"I don't think so."

"Well, then. I can help you, Eve. But each time I do . . . a tiny piece of Minnesota will disappear. Do you mind?"

"What?" The medicated fog in my head must be pretty thick because I have no idea what the hell my telescope is talking about.

"Every time I help you, Eve, a tiny piece of Minnesota will disappear," he repeats.

"Why not a tiny piece of Idaho?"

The sound of his laughter makes the top of my head tingle.

"Okay," he says. "Idaho."

"No, no, Minnesota's fine," I tell him.

He laughs again. "Minnesota it is."

Collage

A tiny piece of
Lidia—her
favorite hair tie—pinned
over the light switch
so not to be
forgotten.

This is how it
began.

For whatever reason,
the hair tie stayed there, joined soon after
by a picture of a swimming pool I cut from
a magazine—I'd always wanted a swimming
pool.

Next came a page
ripped from *The Little Engine*
That Could—a happy group of
fruit and candy.

That night,
the growing collection won

a smile from my mother.
"A collage,"
she noted.

A collage.
Pieces of my life tacked,
taped, and glued onto
the green wall across from
my bed.

After a few years, I began
a second assemblage in the center
of the wall, gluing
two sets of eyes cut from
third-grade school photos—
Lidia's and mine.

"So creepy," Lidia said. But
she laughed. And
I added our noses.

Gradually, I surrounded
the pieces of our faces with
other pieces of us.

Tickets to a
movie my grandparents took us to see,
Lidia's mother's business card

because I didn't know what else
to do with it, a fast food
cup Lidia told me not to touch
when I plucked it from the curb
to throw in the trash. With the germs
already settling in on my hands, I carried it
home and
stapled it to the wall.

The collage surrounding the light fixture
spawned the collage surrounding our eyes
spawned another and another, until
my wall resembled
the effect of multiple rocks
thrown into a green pond, rippling outward.
Each original piece
the sun
in the solar system
of my bedroom wall,
or, as Lidia liked to call it:
"A vertical mess."

She wasn't wrong. Collage wasn't beautiful.
Not in the way a single photograph or
a painting might be. It was clunky, uneven,
and random.

When we jumped to middle school, the

collage jumped to a second wall—
Our seventh-grade algebra homework,
shredded and shellacked.
A ferocious act of release.
A testament to mathematical fortitude.
Art.

Then a spray of notes
passed between us through eighth.
Each scrap
torn apart
words scattered.
We didn't need them whole
to know what we'd said.

Over time, the green paint of my walls
disappeared, and my bedroom became
a world made up of
other worlds made up of
other worlds, so that
my desk, the bed, the telescope, me—
we are all just pieces in the
collage.

Lidia Returns

I WAKE TO THE SOUND OF WIND GUSTS FLAPPING THE LOOSE siding of the old triple-decker. Naked tree branches swing in and out of the square view from my window. A flock of birds flies across a gray morning sky.

They remind me of something. Something I can't remember. A warm feeling of hope flutters in my stomach.

Then I see why.

Lidia is here.

"Hi," I croak, my voice still asleep.

She smiles that Lidia smile that shows up in her eyes even more than on her mouth. "Get your lazy ass out of bed," she says. "You're sleeping the whole goddamn day away."

"I've missed you," I tell her, my eyes watering.

"You're such a fucking wimp." She laughs. Hopping up, she neatly pushes in my desk chair with her one hand, and I remember the other. I remember it all.

"Lid," I whisper. "Lid, I—I'm—"

"Oh, look." She cuts me off, walking over to my window. "It's starting to snow."

Snow?

Minnesota.

I turn to my telescope and silently mouth the words:

Thank you.

Lidia takes one look around my room and gets to work. She stacks my books into a neat pile. She refolds the extra blankets that had slid off the end of my bed. She picks up the dozens of pieces of shredded tissue littering the floor surrounding my bedside, placing them inside one of the three half-empty glasses of water sitting stagnant on my bedside table, all the while complaining about my destructive habit. She's overly familiar with my love of ripping things into tiny pieces so I can build something new out of them later. Just as I'm overly familiar with her extreme love of tidiness. She doesn't miss a single shred.

Lidia, who has cleaned my room a thousand times. Lidia, who I haven't seen for so long. I can't take my eyes from her, or stop smiling, or keep the tears from running down my cheeks and into my pillowcase.

Her job complete, she heads to the kitchen, expertly balancing a pile of dirty dishes and trash. Even though she was born with a single hand, not much ever got in Lidia's way.

Not the cardboard milk cartons from kindergarten that said *Open here*, and never did.

Not the rope that snaked its way thirty feet up to the rafters of the middle school gym.

Not the complex microscopic system of threading a sewing machine, the tedious building of a kinetic sculpture out of toothpicks, the impossible physics of a chin-up bar...not even team sports, where a sweaty symmetrical body seemed a requirement.

Lidia would ache, strain, sweat, boil, grunt, tear, smash, leap, quiver, burn, and bleed before failing to accomplish it all.

Lidia pops her head back into the room.

"Don't fall asleep," she says.

That's your trick, not mine, I think through closed eyes, because she's already gone.

Something I Don't Know

"Lid,"
I whine.
"Lidia, you're sleeping."

It happened every time I slept over.
Lidia would fall asleep
and I'd be left
awake.

"I'm not," she mumbled,
completely sleeping.

"Tell me something I don't know,"
I urged.
"Play the game."

We played this game
all the way through elementary
and into middle school.
Our own version of truth or dare.

Because I knew
everything about her

and she knew
everything about me, the
tiny things we divulged in the dark
were scraped from the sides
of our thoughts. We liked to say
they were the things
that grew our brains
together.

A stolen answer
on a vocab quiz.
An orange penis
discovered in her parents' dresser drawer.
Songs whose lyrics
we ached to think
might one day
be about us.
The thing we wished we'd said
to some jerk,
instead of the thing
we did say.
The shocking discovery of the belt
that went with the penis.

Lying together in the
dark. The walls
as familiar as our skin,
and the warm air a soft cushion

on which to place the
somethings we didn't know
so that everything was
known.
Everything.

"Come on, Lid,"
I complained.
"Play."

Watching her sleep, all
beating heart and breath—free
from being capable, sensible, punctual
Lidia—she became even more beautiful
than she already was.

"Lid," I tried
hopelessly.

"I love you, Eve,"
she whispered
through a final sleepy yawn.

I sighed.
"Tell me something I don't know."

Just Like It Always Was

THE FOUR WALLS OF MY BEDROOM ARE SOMEPLACE. Although where and when seem beside the point. I linger, nested in my bed between my collages. Listening to cars. Listening to birds. Listening to Lidia.

"So," she says, leaning back in my desk chair. "You outta bed yet?"

She notices my Roxy bottle still in my hand and reaches for it. I immediately drop my hand to my side.

"What is it?" she asks. "An antibiotic, or a vitamin to help your spine grow?"

I squeeze the plastic protectively.

"My spine isn't growing," I say, blinking lazily over at her. "It's hardening." I can't believe I'm speaking to her about the surgery. Finally.

"How do you bend after it hardens?" she asks.

"Well, I guess I don't. Or at least not my spine anymore. But they had to glue it together to keep it straight."

"How does the glue dry if it's inside you?"

"It's not really glue. It's the bone from my ribs Dr. Sowah sawed off because they were crushing my heart and lungs. He ground up my rib bones, took out the disks in my spine, and stuck the bony paste in there. Then he attached it all to a couple of long bars with screws as big as my thumb and bolted this whole contraption to a round metal plate attached near my hips." Talking to her about this feels... amazing. Like taking a long hot shower, something I wouldn't be allowed to do for almost four more weeks.

The pain stirs.

"That's gross, Eve," she says. "Are there pictures?"

"There are X-rays somewhere." I open my bottle.

Lidia jumps out of the chair to help me sit up.

"No, don't. It hurts."

"How long do you have to wear this one?" she asks, gesturing to my spinal brace. "It's a lot bigger than your last one."

I shrug like I don't know. But I do know. Sowah said I needed to wear the hard-plastic shell wrapping me from clavicle to hips for four to six months. I haven't figured out whether the time is too short or too long, and so I keep the estimate to myself.

I roll onto my side, wincing.

Lidia moves to grab the water glass on my bedside table.

"Don't bother. I've swallowed it already."

She sighs, shaking her head and looking at me.

My eyes start to water again. I can't stop them.

"Lidia," I whisper.

"Your hair is really greasy," she says, frowning. Ignoring my plea... ignoring the past few horrible weeks.

"I haven't washed it since before the surgery," I confess.

"That was like a month ago," she shrieks in horror.

"Yup," I say, giving her a sleepy smile.

"What about a shower?"

"Nope."

She grimaces and then laughs.

I'm happy to have grossed her out, happy to make her laugh. It's just like it always was.

I settle onto my pillow. I like this part, where I can feel the Roxy in there, battling. I'm panting. And wet with sweat. Though I know soon... very soon... the drug will win.

"How about I get a pot of warm soapy water and wash your hair?"

"It will hurt." But then I give a little snort through my nose because the Roxy is winning, and I know that it won't hurt. Nothing will hurt.

"I'll be careful," she says. "Afterward I'll dry it, and maybe braid it so it doesn't look so messy."

She scooches her chair closer to my bed, chattering on about my hair. I close my eyes and listen, the sound

    of her voice

    opening inside me

    like a beautiful flower in

one of those time-lapse videos.

She is here. With me.

Lidia.

And me.

Me and Lidia.

Me and Lidia

I am dreaming
of the place
where the forsythia grew
lush and green,
branches curving to
create an
entire world.

Our world.

Lidia and me.
Me and Lidia.
Under the forsythia.

Where we
dragged old rugs,
small tables,
cups,
plates,
and anything else no one
would miss.

Where we breathed
each other's air
inside our prehistoric cave,
our hobbit hole,
our home.
Pretending to sleep.
Pretending to eat.
Really eating.
Really playing, checkers,
house,
spy.

In this world
we were the dappled shade, the
sunny yellow blooms, the
soft, brown dirt.
Guarded by the
bending branches from the
curious stares, the
fixed gazes, the
superficial smiles, and
so many trivial, rambling words
whipping round and
round, like wind over mountains,
eroding us.

Under the forsythia,
it was me and Lidia and
me and Lidia. Me and Lidia.
Me and Lidia. MeandLidiaMeandLidiaM
eandLi
dia.

Your Decision

Lying on my back on the living room floor, I attempt
to lift my foot from the yoga mat to meet Nancy's hand for
the millionth time. My toes hover a few inches below her
fingers and then drop to the mat.

Who knew physical therapists came to your home,
ripped you from bed, and forced you to exercise?

I do.

Now.

"Come on, Eve. Give me one more."

I close my eyes and groan as I lift my foot an inch. It's as
much as I can do. It's as much as I want to do. Nancy frowns.
I know this even though my eyes are closed. In the quiet
moment before she speaks, I actually consider the chance
that she may have magically disappeared as per my telescope.

"All right," she says, crushing my fragile hope. The
woman's from Medford, not Minnesota. "Let's get you up."

This hour goes on forever.

Rolling to my side, I bring in my knees and arms the way Nancy taught me, like a baby curling up in a crib, and then climb to all fours. She places my walker in front of me, standing behind it for support. I use it to climb to my feet.

Once I'm up, she looks me over. She does not approve.

"Have you been eating?"

"Yes."

I have not been eating.

"Taking off your brace once a day?"

"Yes."

I've never even considered removing it.

"I know you can't shower yet, Eve," she says, glancing at my grease-matted hair, "but spraying in a bit of dry shampoo, changing into clean pajamas, washing your face. Small efforts at self-care. These are important. Have you looked at yourself in a mirror lately?"

The question stings. No. No, I have not. I have not looked at myself in a mirror. And I don't plan to.

"I mean, gosh, look at your toenails."

Out of instinct, I look down at my toenails. The word *scuzzy* comes to mind.

"But I can't reach them anymore," I say, which is the truth, though I'd never thought to try.

She nods. And I can see she feels a bit sheepish for pointing it out. "Well, we can talk to your mom about them. Have you been practicing laps with your forearm crutches?" she asks, changing the subject.

"Yes."

It's another lie.

"Let's try it together." She hands me the crutches and we walk around the dining room table like it's the track that circles the football field at school. The laps quickly take their toll and I struggle to disguise my ragged breath while hoping she doesn't notice the sweat running down the sides of my forehead, both indicators of my extreme sedentary existence.

Nancy is quiet while we walk. Like she's thinking. And that can't be good for me. I need to get her off my back. Literally.

"Next week we start stairs, right?" I ask, breaking the quiet and giving myself a chance to gulp in some much-needed oxygen. "I suppose we'll be taking it one step at a time," I add, attempting to break her concentration.

It works. She cracks a rare smile.

"Just be thankful your apartment is on the first floor, and you've only got three steps to the front door," she says, leading me to the couch.

I have no interest in the front door. Except to see Nancy use it as soon as possible.

After almost an hour of pulling on colorful exercise bands and trotting about the house, my energy level is below empty. The plate, bars, and screws bolting me together may all be made of titanium, a low-density metal, but right now it feels as if Sowah used a few of those U-shaped bike locks to fuse me.

My mother sweeps into the room. She tries to give me a warm pat on my arm, but it comes out more like she's pressing a button for an elevator. At least she's holding a glass of water.

It's Roxy time.

"How's the patient doing?" she asks.

"Well, Susan," Nancy says. "The truth is, Eve hasn't been progressing as fast as I think she should be, and I'm concerned about her personal hygiene."

I roll my eyes at poor Nancy's attempt to engage with my mother's question. My physical therapist still doesn't realize my mother is never looking for an answer—the question is the beginning and end of her effort.

While Nancy yaks away, my mother stares at her moving lips with raised eyebrows and wide-open eyes. This is how my mother impersonates "listening." She can't do the real thing, not that Nancy notices; no one ever does. My eyes lock on the forgotten orange bottle in my mother's hand.

"So...I think we should increase my visits from two times a week to three times a week."

My groan of despair is so loud it surprises even me, and I grab my rib cage as if it was the source of my grief. The sawed-off ribs do hurt like hell, so this one isn't a complete lie.

My mother's eyes light up. I can tell she sees my suffering as an escape from Nancy.

"Oh, sweetheart, give Nancy another minute and then you can settle into bed and rest for a while," she says, lobbing the ball into Nancy's court. Will my therapist allow me to wallow in anguish just to finish her report? I see now that it's probably the whole reason my mother brought my Roxy out here in the first place—to dangle my pain in front of Nancy so she'd leave—because it's Thursday, and that means my mother has her weekly dinner with Mary Fay.

"No, no," Nancy says, tucking her tablet away and bending to collect her tools of torture—the bands from hell and her giant red ball. "It's time I hit the road."

My mother opens the orange bottle, and my heart warms.

"Soon you won't be needing that," Nancy says, nodding her chin toward my Roxy. "See you Tuesday."

I choke down the pill as she closes the door.

Soon? How soon? Two months? One?

Not that soon.

I want my bed.

I think about washing my face or changing into clean sweatpants. But not really. Really, it just feels good to be angry at Nancy for making these suggestions, and the anger gives me the energy to clomp across the living room toward my bedroom.

"I'll be home by ten," my mother says. "I left the second bottle of Roxanol next to a glass of water on your nightstand. Call if you need anything." She doesn't say *Call if you need me.* Anyway, she knows I won't call.

"You good, Eve?" she asks.

I stop at the door to my room. I know she isn't looking for a real answer, but I can't help myself.

"I don't know? Nancy seems to believe I'm not progressing. Maybe we should talk about it."

"Well, your physical therapist can show up two times, three times, or even ten times a week, but your personal effort is the key. And that's your decision, isn't it?" Speech over, she leaves.

My decision.

My mother decrees everything my decision. I can remember being four years old and hearing that how many cookies I ate was my decision. My decision was a lot of cookies. At six, quitting dance at Miss Elaine's was my decision. The amount of screen time I engaged in? My decision. How late I stayed up? My decision. Sleepover on a school night? My decision. Grades, sex, drugs? Really just grades and drugs but, still, all . . . my decision.

Fuck her for always putting everything on me.

I fling my walker into my desk and it knocks shit everywhere. I roll onto my bed, defeated.

Those cookies were my last good decision.

Something I Already Knew

That night
half asleep,
Lidia told me
something I already knew.
"I want a hand,"
and my decision
was to say
nothing.

But I wasn't
doing nothing,
I was doing
something.
I was hoping
that in the silent passing seconds
she'd actually fallen asleep.

"Sometimes," Lidia
said, followed by a
swish of covers—she was
not asleep—
"I feel it."

She stared up
at the ceiling. The moonlight
shining through the window,
casting a shadow—her eyelashes
dark and feathery
against her bedroom wall.

"You know?"
she whispered.

I didn't answer.
But I did know.
Having
that second hand.
Having
that straight spine.
Looking
like everyone else.
Being
like everyone else—some days
it all seemed like it should be so
simple.

"I'm going to put it on my Christmas list."

Funny. A hand on a Christmas list.
We were almost thirteen, and
no longer believed in Santa.

But I didn't laugh.
I didn't do anything, and all the things
I wasn't doing, wasn't saying
added up, and she
scooched closer,
our noses inches apart.

"They won't get me one.
They said some online
rubber hand is silly, and
I don't need it."
They were her parents.

Her eyes asked,
What do you think?

I think...
Lidia's parents were being just like
Lidia:
practical.
Although with this hand thing,
Lidia wasn't being very
practical.

"Eve?"

"Sorry," I said, closing my eyes,
so I couldn't see

hers,
accusing me of being
just
like
them.
Parents.
Doctors.
PTs.
Everyone with hands.
Everyone who wasn't her.

And through the quiet,
I felt it.
She was thinking
about my spine.

My eyes flew open.
"What?"

"Nothing," she said.

"Something," I said.

She tossed her body to face away
from me and pulled
the covers up over her shoulders.
After she made sure she couldn't
see my face, she spit out that something.

"You could be straight
if you wanted."

I knew it.
I knew it was this.

What I didn't know was
why it hurt so badly, those words.
Why they made me hotter than hot. So that my crooked
    bones
felt like they were searing through my skin,
burning the whole of me to white ash.

She fell asleep,
while I was on fire,
leaving me to cool in the dark.

*You could be straight
if you wanted.*

Sawed open.
Rearranged.
Stapled shut.

Pain

It's dark.

I'm tangled. I need my meds. Fucking Nancy and her fucking PT.

I can't turn. I'm pinned to the bed. Godfuckingdamnit, I need my medicine.

Mom, I mouth without sound, like a goldfish...then I remember her speech, the door closing.

I throw my body to the side and the pain shoves its fist down my throat, choking me.

I want OUT. Out of this bed. Out of this brace. Out of this body.

Desperate, I tear at the sheet and roll for the Roxy. The pain attacks again, sinking its metal teeth into my stomach.

The feeling suffocates me and I fall back, trying to catch my breath.

Because there is only one way out of this, I roll with everything I have toward the orange bottle.

Managing to make it to my side, my body shaking and wet, my nose smashed up against my pillow and my own hot breath slamming my face over and over again, I reach out and grab for the bottle, knocking it to the floor.

Help. Help me. Someone help me.

She's got to be home.

The bell.

Clutching it, I jerk it about. Its only sound is a dull clang. I switch it to my left hand, but my fingers are too sweaty and shaky to hold it by the knob at the top—and the pain is coming again, it's coming again. Hugging my plastic-covered body, I close my eyes and groan in fear as the attack approaches.

Lunging, it tears into me, ripping me apart until pain zings out of my eyes like lasers. I gasp, holding back the sobs.

Working the bell's knob into my fist, I slam it against the bed and am rewarded with a clear ring. I slam it again. And again. And again. Ringing the bell over and over and over until it slips away and flies out of my hand, hitting the floor with one last clang.

She isn't coming.

No one is coming.

I clutch at my blankets, shoving my face into their hotness. It hurts too much, nothing should hurt this much.

The force of the vomit rolls me to the side of the bed. It pours from me in gusts. Onto my bed. Onto my floor. Onto the bottle of Roxy.

Hanging from the bed, I snatch up the wet bottle and roll back, clutching it against my heart while the pain eats me alive.

Cracking it open with one hand, I pinch out a pill.

I'm not supposed to chew it, but I don't give a shit right now.

I stick my thumb into the bottle to keep my precious Roxy from spilling out over my sweat-soaked sheets while I swallow lumps of chalky medicine mixed with the sour taste of vomit.

My body rasps out a gag. And another.

Shit!

Opening my eyes as wide as possible, I try to unglue myself from my body, like I can somehow project my brain onto the ceiling of my room until my stomach has ingested this pill.

"Eve," he calls.

I groan to shut him up—it hurts to hear.

Seconds seem like minutes. Minutes. Years.

Why isn't it working?

Crying is like blood in the water to the pain, but I can't hold it back anymore. I'm breaking down.

"Six more minutes," he soothes, "and you'll feel better."

"I'm dying," I shout into my pillow, my mouth full of spit and tears and chunks of Roxy.

"It's working," he says in his thick, calming voice.

"No," I gasp, "no, no, no." But the pulsing pain and I are slowly separating.

He is right.
Right.
Right.
Right.

"Better?"

His voice is soft in my ears, making me sink deeper into my bed.

"Will I ever be?" I ask, panting and wet with sweat and not looking or caring for an answer.

"Telescopes see the past, Eve," he says. "Not the future."

The past?

I hear the echoing crowds of the mall. Giant green-leaved plants. The smell of popcorn. And the pain. Not the brutal, searing kind of being sliced through with a sharp blade, but the extraordinarily aching kind where every atom of you attempts to split. The kind you can't chew your way out of. Or can you?

And so I chew.

Again. Shivering. Cold.

"What about Minnesota?"

He answers
with a tinge of pink
behind my eyelids,
a warm spot in the center of my chest

that grows...and grows
until my hands are warm.
My feet are warm.
I am warm.
Because it is summer,
of course.

The Burger Hut

We were fourteen
that July,
and therefore eligible
for our first jobs.

The Burger Hut needed
two people willing
to dress as a
hamburger and french fry.

She was totally willing.
Because it meant money
for the hand.

I was totally willing.
Because it meant dressing up
as food.

Lidia studied the Burger Hut's history.
We watched training videos on YouTube.
Then she suggested we memorize
the Burger Hut Mission.

That is going too far,
I said.
She laughed.

At the interview
I stood, hunched, next to
the deep fryer with my hands at my sides,
my eyes forward,
sweating,
like a guilty suspect in a lineup.

Lidia answered the questions
glancing at me
as if I was in on it all.

She wore
long sleeves. I wore
many yards of fabric over
hard plastic.
She still had one hand.
I was still crooked as hell.
This wasn't going to work.

But then
Lidia placed her hand on her heart.
I did the same.

And together,
we recited the Burger Hut Mission
as if it were the Pledge of Allegiance.

We got the job.

"Lidia"

"LIDIA?"

"Lid?"

"Stop talking, you're moving your feet."

Her voice is muffled down at the end of my bed where she is painting my toenails.

"Lidia."

"Eve, you're killing me."

I pick up my foot. "Is that red? I thought I said blue."

"Blue makes your feet look veiny."

"Are my feet veiny?"

"Stop moving."

I slowly turn my head to face my telescope, wondering if Lidia considers this moving. Dust sparkles around him in the sunbeams like it can't settle on something so darkly beautiful. He brought her. To me.

"Lidia?"

"Eve!"

"No, I was going to say something."

"What?" she asks, sitting up from my feet and glaring at me. But it's her loving glare.

"Well?" she asks.

"Now I forgot."

She lets out a frustrated huff and returns to my toes.

I didn't really have anything to say. Besides her name. Which she knew.

The sun is shining into the room. Another day. Here. Inside. Staring at my collages moving like snakes across my walls.

Outside, in the world, things may be happening. Cars driving. People working. Clouds drifting. Trees growing. But in here, all is still. The only sound is the soft murmuring of Mary Fay and my mother working together out in the living room.

"Remember the Burger Hut, Lidia?"

"Why are you thinking about that dump?" she says, her hot breath tickling my feet.

"It wasn't a dump," I say.

She doesn't answer.

"Lidia?"

"Eve! Really?"

Oh my god. Did I just say it again?

"I'm so fucking sorry, Lid. It just slipped out." I laugh. I can't help it. I laugh and laugh and it sounds like I'm laughing inside an empty tuna fish can.

"'The Burger Hut promises…,'" I say, positioning myself for the pledge.

She jams the nail polish wand into the bottle and shakes her head no.

"'…every burger will be the most delicious charbroiled burger,'" I continue in a solemn manner, "'ever to be flipped on a grill.'"

"'To be joined…,'" she grumps. She can't help herself, and we finish strong. "'…*by the crispiest fries. The iciest drink. The cleanest table. In the happiest of huts.*'"

The doorbell rings.

My mother's voice. Speaking Spanish.

Thomas Aquinas is here.

She always has to do that, annoyingly practice her awful Spanish the second she sees him.

His deep voice speaking slowly and clearly has me immediately pull the sheet up closer to my chin while I do not picture him standing twenty feet away from me on the front steps, in one of his yellow T-shirts, his long dark hair tied back, that old jean jacket, his thick wrists—

The front door closes.

I hear my mother walk into the living room and off into the kitchen.

Then, silence.

I do not look down at her.

"He brought my homework."

"Hmm," she says.

"School Within a School program partner. He has to."

"Hmm," she says again.

I rummage for a Roxy and then turn my head to change my view. To change my thoughts. My hair scratching against the pillow. Blinking up at the ceiling, I try to sigh without moving.

"Lidia?"

She doesn't answer.

"You forgot your hand during the pledge," I say.

"Are you sure you want to talk about hands?" she asks.

I close my eyes. Because my head hurts from the throbbing in my back, my hips, my heart.

The Hand

The hand was due to arrive
by UPS
at any moment.
Maybe this moment. Multiple
sketchy
tracking numbers
making it impossible to
know.

Our chins bobbed to attention
at the sound of every
motor sloshing over
wet road.
Though Lidia and I
both knew
the sound we sought was the
slow, low rumble
of a
large brown truck.

Keeping it secret
from her parents

meant the hand would
ship to me.

Cosmetic hand prosthetics
custom made of
silicone,
the website read.
Cosmetic.
As if a hand was the same as
longer eyelashes or
redder lips.

Another motor.
Another car.
It was late.
It would not
be today.

So Lidia
went home, but
I stayed
at the big picture window.
Waiting.
Dreaming.
Of it arriving
when Lidia was absent
because I
loved imagining

the moment
I'd call and shout,
Your hand is here!

There's always a difference, though,
between the imagined moment
and the real one.

The Real One

You were cranky.
I wasn't ready when you pulled up.
"As usual."

But god, Lid,
you knew how hard it was to
wrap a body in a brace.
But I know
slow can be frustrating.
Slow can suck.

Plus,
it was New Year's Day and that meant
no box—so no hand, leaving us
no choice but to head to the mall
to spend the day looking for—
sigh,
hats.

You were going through a hat phase.
You were always going through
some phase.
The slippers-as-shoes phase.

The two-pairs-of-socks-at-once phase.
The wild-patterned-tights phase. And now
the very long-running
hat phase.

That morning
you were wearing a hat
I'd never seen before.
A little black fedora.

You caught me eyeballing it as I
struggled into the passenger seat
of your rusty Toyota.
"Respect the hat," you said,
completely aware of the shade
I was throwing.

Okay—so you looked
fucking adorable in it.
Maybe this was why
I hated the hats.
Because you looked
so good in them.

Hat, cute skirt, and
your usual—
an oversize hoodie to
hide the hand you didn't have.

Along with my ankle boots
you'd borrowed a year ago and were
never planning on returning.

You looked good in those, too.
You looked good in everything,
because your bones weren't
twisting in circles like
some sort of lazy river.

I also wore my usual—
overalls to hide my brace
on the inside of my clothing.

Was it a better look
than wearing my plastic shell
on the outside?
Probably not,
but it made me feel better. Even if between
the clasps of the overalls and
the Velcro straps of the brace, I had to
regulate my liquid intake
because stripping down to pee
in a public restroom was
seriously impossible.

Before you pulled from the curb,
you reached into your lap and

brought forth a floppy knit visor.
For me.

This was not your
first attempt to
bring me on board
with your hat phase. But it
was the first time I
stuck one of those hats
on my head.

I needed to tell you
something I hadn't told you.
Something I should have told you
six months earlier.
Something I should have told you
right then, sitting in the car.

But when you clapped your hands
in corny glee
at the sight of me in that
silly visor—
I couldn't.
For the same reason
I hadn't told you
all the hundreds of times
I'd meant to.

Because it hurt to
wipe away your joy, Lid,
for any reason.
But especially
for this reason.

Eve and the Serpent

I'M NOT AWAKE. OR ASLEEP. I'M SOMEWHERE IN BETWEEN.

I like it here.

Suspended.

———

"How are you tonight, Miss Abbott?" he asks. His voice is soft inside my ears. I like it when he calls me Miss Abbott. Although I like it even more when he calls me Eve.

"I am..." But I really don't know how I am, so I just return his question. "How are you, sir?"

He does that bowing thing, where he tips the large eye of the telescope down toward my rug. "I am always well when I'm with you."

My telescope is so nice.

I sigh.

"Yes, Eve?" he asks, making every hair on my head

tingle. He doesn't move but seems to breathe in slowly, ready to absorb all I'm about to say.

"I am . . . wondering about my spine."

"Nineteen degrees," he says.

"Nineteen degrees," I repeat. "Fifty-seven degrees closer to zero than I was before. And I hope . . . I hope that it looks straight. I think I can feel it, you know? I think I feel the straightness."

He doesn't respond, and now all I feel is trapped, alone, in some hot place . . . and hoping? For what?

"Never mind," I mumble, reaching into my drawer and riffling about for a Roxy. I've hidden a nest of them in an old sock so the empty bottle would prompt my mother to refill the prescription.

Sucking up a bit of spit, I swallow. It'll take more than a Roxy to bring me back to the cool, suspended place—it'll take a Roxy and ten minutes. And before the seconds can tick by, fear flutters in my chest. Who am I now? Like this. I don't want it anymore.

Arthritis. Osteoporosis. Kyphosis. Lordosis. Spondylolisthesis. Impaired mobility. Diminished lung capacity. Enlarged heart. Early death. These are real. Real results of staying crooked. And anyway, it's too late.

Too late.

"Say something," I beg.

In the quiet seconds that follow, the fear whips itself into anger. "Say something, you shitty lump of plastic." The words rush out of me, sucking the breath along with them, my heart beating against its hard shell. Because I'm talking to a telescope. A goddamn telescope.

He remains silent.

But the anger is a flash. It sizzles and disappears. Or maybe it's the Roxy slowly taking effect. Smoothing out the wrinkles inside me. And in the emptiness, the darkness, my heart slows to a thump.

"You're not shitty," I whisper.

He laughs. And the happy sound soaks through my skin. The minutes have added up. And with them, my thoughts drift off in another direction.

"So . . . who are you, really?"

"A shitty lump of plastic?" he says.

"Or . . . the devil," I suggest.

"So ambitious."

"You did make that pact with me. Remember?"

"Minnesota," he says. "Of course I remember, Eve."

The drug is filling me with every good feeling in the world—he is filling me with every good feeling in the world.

"What's it like being pure evil?" I ask.

"Is the devil pure evil?"

"He made hell, didn't he?" I say.

"Did he? I thought god was the creator."

"Hmm. Interesting," I murmur. "I'd think about this if I could think."

"Yes," he says, "the Roxy."

"Why do you say it like that . . . *the Roxy*?" First Nancy, and now him. Everybody just thinks they can talk about my Roxy.

My mouth feels hot and I wish I had enough strength to sit up and drink the glass of water sitting next to my bed, and then I wish that not only did I have the strength to sit up and drink it, but that it had ice floating in it, a lot of ice . . . and that it was an orange soda.

"Eve."

"Listen, I'm tired and want to sleep. If you are some old snake *come to tempt Eve*," I say, using my fingers to air quote it, although they're under my covers so I'm not sure why I do this, "you should forgive my lack of politeness."

"Although if I am the Serpent, Eve, forgiveness really wouldn't be my thing."

I can't hold back a sleepy smile—and once again the sound of his voice erases my anger like waves erase footprints from sand, and an overwhelming feeling of needing to touch him washes over me. I reach out, but he's just beyond my fingertips. I close my eyes and imagine his sleek coolness, my mind stretching out flat and comfortable. Outside the wind whistles and moans.

"March." I sigh. "In like a lion, out like a lamb." A quote my second-grade teacher, Miss Fuller, taught us.

"It's February, Eve."

Miss Fuller had us team up with a partner. One of us had to draw the lion and the other the lamb. Lidia picked the lion. So I drew the lamb.

A gust of wind strikes the house, rattling the windows.

But I'm warm. Very warm. And safely wrapped in my staples and plastic with my Roxy pulsing through me.

"You don't like the cold," I say.

"I don't?"

"Because you're the devil."

"Oh, right."

"That's why you wanted Minnesota to disappear."

"No, Eve, you wanted Minnesota to disappear."

His words send a shiver through me.

"Ah, but the devil is a liar," I point out through a large yawn.

"If the devil were truly evil, Eve, he'd tell the truth."

Lies, Lies, Lies

Waiting for Bogdani to begin
class, I felt a tapping
on my brace. A very familiar
tapping.

Thomas Aquinas.

"I do not answer people who knock on me."
A lie.

Next, I felt him scribbling.
"You best not be drawing on me."

"Es
un gato,
Eve," he said.
"Everybody loves
cats."

Though I agreed with this,
of course, I'd
never admit it to
Thomas Aquinas.

His real name was Thomas Aquino,
though due to this being Boston, a
seriously Catholic town,
everybody called him Thomas Aquinas
after the saint.

Thomas Aquinas was no
saint,
but he was
brilliant.
He could easily be valedictorian next year,
if he ever did any work or
wasn't murdered first, which was entirely possible
since Thomas Aquinas was also
an asshole.

No one liked him.
Not the teachers
because he was a smart-ass.
Not the students
because he was a smart-ass.
Not Lidia
because she said he was always
around.
Me?

"Eve."

We lived two doors apart on
Wrentham Street off
Dorchester and
we were
partners in the
School Within a School system,
a program in our large
high school that
functioned like a buddy system.

"Eve."

Four.
Years.

"Hey, Eve."

Same.
Buddy.

Which meant I saw
an awful lot of
Thomas Aquinas
and
did an awful lot of
SWAS assignments,
since he never did
shit.

"Eve."

The sound of
Thomas Aquinas
saying my name
a fourth time
tweaked my last nerve, and I
cursed the alphabet,
my surname, and the universe—the
trifecta of causes for this miserable
pairing—and with my
judgment clouded
by his warm breath
on my neck,
I spun to face him.

"Good morning, gorgeous." He
smiled over the top of his gold-rimmed
professor glasses, which perfectly matched his
dark intense stare, yet
always looked out of place
framed by long,
dirty hair, colorful
sleeve tattoos,
and one of the same ratty T-shirts
he wore every single day,
which read *Gophers*.

"I noticed you missed the last SWAS assignment,"
he said.

"I did not."
A lie.

"That's unlike you, Eve. Let
me know if you need help,"
he said.

"I do not."
A lie.

"And by help,
I don't mean with anything
SWAS related,"
he said,
winking.

Winking!

"Stop talking to me."

"'Your success is my success is our success,'"
he said, reciting
the SWAS motto.

I ignored him.

"Big surgery coming up next week.
Don't worry. I've got your back."

I ignored him.

"Get it, Eve? Your back?"

I ignored him.

"I just love our morning chats."
He sighed.

I hated them.
A lie.

Everything I Want

SIX WEEKS OUT FROM SURGERY AND I'VE MADE IT AS FAR AS the living room couch. I had my mother place the telescope in front of the big picture window before she left for work. One nice thing about having a parent not ultra-interested in your life is they don't ask inane questions like *Why do you need me to drag a telescope into the living room for the day?*

I sip the last of my lukewarm tea while I gaze at it.

"You really like that thing," Lidia says.

"I do," I tell her. "He gives me everything I want."

She laughs at my silly-sounding response, which warms me more than the tea.

Having Lidia back makes me feel like I'm ten years old. I feel so good. Although I doubt I look it. My hair is supergreasy. My face is paler than the whiteboards at school. I'm wearing the same torn red snowflake pajamas I first put on when I got home from the hospital. And except when the nurse visits, I haven't removed my brace once. I've also lost a bunch of weight. Too much weight. Being skinny may be the dream of most sixteen-year-old girls, but when your bones look like a game of pick-up sticks, having them more on display is never the goal.

"Your toenails are gross, Eve. Let me paint them."

I look down at my feet. She's right.

"Red, they'd look really good red," she suggests.

"Um—" I say. Something feels wrong. I'm not sure what.

"I know," she cuts me off. "You like blue better."

"No, Lid," I whisper. "I don't like blue."

We hear the front door open, followed by a whip of cold air. Lidia stands up. "I'll get the polish," she says, as she slips off into my bedroom just as my mother walks into the living room followed by . . .

Thomas Aquinas?

My head is ripped from its Roxy haze as I scoot below the couch throw. Pain from the thoughtless movement zings through the trunk of my body.

"I bumped into your pal Thomas on the way in, Eve," my mother says.

Thomas Aquinas grins from behind her. He's holding a stack of work for me.

"Thomas is not my pal," I say. "He's my partner."

Instantly, I hear what this sounds like and quickly add, "For SWAS. My partner for SWAS."

And then because I *know* my mother will not know what SWAS is, and I don't want her asking in front of Thomas, I throw in, "You know, the School Within a School program."

"Well, he's also a June Jordan fan," my mother informs me, not at all interested in what I just said. "And is considering a double major in poetry and women's studies in college." She's the head of the English Department at Franklin Community College.

"A women's studies major?" I ask. This is just like my mother, to know more about the neighbor kid than she does about me.

"Yes, and trust me, Eve, I've heard all the jokes," Thomas says. He always has to annoyingly say my name.

"I don't know any jokes."

I sound a bit like an asshole, though I don't mean to. I really just don't know any jokes.

His eyes narrow, like he can't figure me out. The easy hatred we share at school seems to be missing with him standing in my living room.

"Anyway," he says, "you look busy."

He turns toward my mother. "Nice seeing you again, Dr. Abbott."

"No, no, she's not busy. Siéntate. Siéntate."

"Mom." Oh my god, I hate my mother.

She ignores me. "Eve's a huge June Jordan fan, too."

I am not a June Jordan fan. I barely know who June Jordan is. We had to read a book of her poetry last year in AP English and my mother noticed it in my hands one day. Since then, she regularly refers to me as a lover of June Jordan. She and Mary Fay both teach at Franklin, my mother poetry and gender and Mary Fay poetry and African American studies. My mother has been dreaming of my future as a poetry major since she saw that book under my arm. I've stopped trying to correct her. Once something crawls into my mother's head, it stays locked in there forever, like a prisoner without hope of parole.

My mother takes off down the hall...leaving Mr. Women's Studies standing in our living room. He shifts his weight from foot to foot, glancing around. I've never seen an uncomfortable Thomas Aquinas. He looks...*softer* without a smirk.

"Thanks for bringing my work."

"Part of the job," he says, and then adds, "partner."

I squirm under the tiny blanket. I knew he'd caught that. Seeing through people is Thomas Aquinas's goddamn superpower.

"You can just toss it there," I suggest in a breezy way, jerkily using my chin to point out the dining room table, and totally knowing he probably caught this as well.

"Which is just where I found it a couple of days ago, minus any completed work," he says. "But the joy is in the journey, right, Eve?"

I decide to cough a few times in order to let that comment pass. I figure Thomas Aquinas doesn't know you don't cough after spinal surgery. Anyway, I could have a cold. Or pneumonia. Lots of people get pneumonia after surgery. I hope I don't have pneumonia.

He places the books on the table and walks back into the living room.

"So, Eve." He clears his throat. "You like poetry?"

His hair is out of its ponytail and is falling across his shoulders, and dark stubble has grown out all over his face. He has large features—wide eyes, a big nose, a big forehead, and his hands are big, too. He just looks...bigger standing inside my house.

"Not really."

Again, I sound like an assole, though I'm totally not trying to.

He nods and laughs a little.

"And I guess you don't like astronomy either?" he asks, glancing at my telescope.

My breath catches at the mention of my telescope. "I just started using it," I say, which is pretty much true.

He folds his arms across his chest and looks into my eyes. Waiting. Maybe for me to offer some sort of star information?

My mind spins like it's in orbit, but besides this, I have nothing.

"So, what about those Rockets?" Thomas says.

I stare at him, lost. Can you see rockets through a telescope?

"The college's hockey team," he explains. "And I'm just teasing you, Eve. I thought talking sports might help the conversation since this is Boston. I was obviously wrong."

The mention of hockey reminds me of Minnesota's wiki page, which I've been staring at for the past few days, and before I can stop myself, I ask, "Do you like hockey?"

Thomas looks at me, trying to figure out if I'm being serious. Then he straight out asks: "Are you joking?"

"No," I whisper.

"Really," he mumbles, unfolding his arms and opening his jean jacket wide and pointing at his shirt. It's the same yellow shirt he wears every day of his life, but I read it for the first time.

Gophers Hockey.

My eyes widen at what it says underneath that.

Minnesota.

"Do you follow hockey?" he asks.

"I follow Minnesota," I say.

"The Wild?"

I guess the blank look I give him is a little frustrating.

"The Wild is Minnesota's professional hockey team," he says, sucking in a big breath through his obnoxiously large nose. But I can't take my eyes off that word on his chest.

"So...pleasure, as always, Eve." And he dips his head at me like we're in some 1950s movie or something. "I hope you feel better. Text me if you have questions on any of the work. I did all the SWAS shit. Figured I owed you a few of these after, you know, the last two and a half years of letting you do it all. I'll be back with more work next week, unless you need something before then."

"I won't," I say, a little too fast. "Need anything," I add, at a much more normal speed. "But thanks."

He looks back at me, and we stare at each other until my stomach rises into my chest. My mother walks into the living room carrying files under one arm and my Roxy in the other, saving me.

"Going so soon?" she asks, handing me a Roxy, which I gulp down with a swig from one of the many glasses of water that litter the coffee table, though I'm pretty sure I've recently self-medicated. She hasn't taken off her coat and is obviously running back to work.

"Sizable load of homework tonight," he says, throwing me a snarky smile. Ah. There's the Thomas Aquinas I know.

Placing my bottle down on the coffee table, she walks to the front door and Thomas Aquinas opens it for her.

"I'll be home right after my evening class," my mother says.

Thomas Aquinas salutes me and then shuts the door behind them.

The sound of the closing door fades, and my ears ring with the emptiness. After a few minutes, I think that maybe Thomas Aquinas and his shirt were just a dream...until Lidia mimics his voice. "'Pleasure, as always, Eve,'" she says. "That kid is just plain strange. He thinks everyone is a fool but him."

"Yeah," I say. "But...I did kind of look like a fool."

Lidia laughs. "Who cares. It's Thomas Aquinas."

"Right," I say, staring out the front window and picturing him walking down Wrentham in his jean jacket.

Out of the corner of my eye, I see Lidia pick up my Roxy and walk across the living room to the gold armchair. Flopping into it, she examines the orange bottle.

"What are you doing?" I ask.

"I'm not doing anything," she says, turning the bottle around and around in her hand.

She keeps studying it, her dark eyes growing darker against the natural paleness of her face.

"What's wrong? Is there something wrong?" I ask.

"Nothing's wrong, Eve. I was just looking at it. Are you feeling okay?"

She's still looking at the bottle. Not at me.

"I just need my medicine."

I say it harder than I mean to. And I'm out of breath, which I try to hide, I don't know why.

Lidia sighs, and that tiny little pushing out of air filled with disapproval gathers in my chest. "It seems like you need it a lot, Eve."

That's all it takes.

"Yeah, well, I've just been through an eleven-hour surgery and had metal rods and a plate welded into me, and half my left rib cage sawed off."

I watch her face. It has a look on it. A look that says, *I win, always, because all I need to do is just sit here. And you lose.*

"Problem?" I ask. Trying to hold on. Trying not to fall into her trap. But it's too hot inside me, a burning pressure expanding, shoving at my casings, and it's all I can do to keep myself from screeching.

"Forget it, Eve."

Forget it?

Forget it just means fuck you. It means this is your shit, not mine, thank god, and I can just leave you like this, all balled up and pissier than pissed sitting in your own piss.

That is what it means.

Forget it.

And I don't fucking *forget it*. I hold it inside and let it twist itself into knot after knot after knot, filling my belly, smashing my heart against my sternum, forcing itself up my throat and into my skull, until it threatens to explode out the top of my head. But it doesn't. I won't let it out. I won't let her have this one.

She slaps the orange plastic bottle on the table next to me.

I don't dare touch that bottle. Instead, I close my eyes, and despite the raging storm whipping through me, I say it, calmly, quietly.

"Make her disappear."

I sit, frozen,
clutching at the round, smooth plastic
of my Roxy bottle. Knowing
I've been here before.

The Real One

You wore the fedora.
I wore the visor when,
two hours later, wandering
under the bright lights of the mall,
I finally let it fall
from my mouth.
"I'm having the surgery."

I remember the
single word that slipped
from yours.
"What?"

Not a happy and excited
WHAT?
But something much smaller,
tighter.

I looked away to give you time—
instantly feeling your anger at this.
Me,
giving you
time.

Me,
knowing you needed it.
Knowing you needed something.

"Two weeks from now,"
I whispered,
watching you
out of the corner of my eye while you
tried to breathe,
tried to respond.
All you managed was a
lick of your lips.

It started then. My babbling.
Anything to cut through
the terrible silence.

Blood draws
MRIs
pulmonary function tests
out of school
for the rest of January and February
and maybe March
better junior year because
college apps
you know
and just think

Thomas the saint will have to do
all the work for
School Within a Freakin' School, you're so lucky, Lid,
to be partnered with Ayanna Bilkowski
that chick works harder than a Navy SEAL
maybe harder—

"You're having the surgery?"
you asked,
sounding
more like I needed you
to sound. Like I
wished you'd
wanted to sound.

"January fourteenth," I said,
forcing my mouth
into the shape
of a smile, and struggling
to hold it there.

Then... *finally*
you threw your arms
around me
and I hoped more than anything
you couldn't feel me panting.

"Good for you, Eve," you said,
your voice vibrating off the plastic shell
of my brace. "You're going to be straight, and
I'm going to have two hands."

You said it like we were going someplace.
But not the same place.

Need

When I wake up, it's dark. I'm still on the couch. Still holding my Roxy. It takes less than a second for the fight with Lidia to flood my memory.

I turn my face toward the window. Close my eyes. Try to breathe slower. Try to return to wherever I was—that quiet, soft place of unconsciousness. But I've crossed some sort of awareness line and it won't let me back in.

I open my eyes. The light coming in from the bay window illuminates the living room. The streetlight throws a stretched-out square across the living room rug and onto the dining room table, where a stack of books and papers sits.

Schoolwork.

In my mind's eye I see Thomas Aquinas standing in my living room, wearing his T-shirt from Minnesota. I see him opening up his jacket, showing me the words *Gophers Hockey*. And before I can stop myself, excitement crackles across my chest as I remember how nicely those letters stretched across his.

Then I remember another boy. This one in a black fedora, and I pluck out a pill, stick it in my mouth—swallowing it with a sip from the nearest glass of water. It's warm. And I can taste the dust floating on the top of it. I have no idea how long it's been sitting there.

I settle back to concentrate on the Roxy's effect, absently reaching my fingers into the orange bottle to count my pills. Then I cap it and close my eyes while the dwindling number settles heavily at the bottom of my stomach.

The blanket is twisted around my legs.

And it's hot.

If only the window were open. I ache for fresh air. I close my eyes and imagine it.

"As you wish," he whispers.

Cold air slides across my face. My god it feels good.

"So did I just wipe out a few lakes in return for my breeze?" I ask.

"You've visited Minnesota's wiki page," he says.

"'The land of ten thousand lakes.'" I recite Minnesota's nickname, sucking in a huge breath of state-destroying air, drawing it in long and slow. It tastes cold and delicious—yet by the time I'm releasing that very same breath, I see her on the chair, her eyes on my Roxy.

"Take me back," I whisper, meaning exactly that. Back. To being twisted and bent and hunched and me. Me. How could I have wanted to be anything but what I was? Now

I am...this. And I don't know what this is. It's like Sowah straightened my spine but left everything else crooked.

"I can stop the pain," he says.

"Yes," I beg him. "Please."

"She didn't need the hand, Eve."

My telescope. It's scary how he understands me.

"Do I need you?" I ask.

He laughs. The sound tingles across my scalp.

But then I see her face...the disapproving look.

I pull out my phone. And text.

Lidia

And then wait, staring at the screen, staring at all the bubbles filled with her name. **Lidia Lidia**

There is never an answer. She is never going to answer.

"Eve," he says quietly, kindly. "You can stop the pain."

He's right. I can.

I dig out another pill. This time, I don't give a shit how many are left. Though of course I know how many are left. Exactly how many. Not enough.

An emptiness fills me...if that is even possible, to be filled by nothing.

"She didn't need it," he repeats. Although that sentence doesn't comfort me the way it did two minutes ago.

Why was the hand something we could share, but not the surgery?

The Surgery

That morning felt
more like I was starring
in a movie
of my life, not actually
living it.

I couldn't stop
narrating
myself.

"Take a shower, Eve.
Scrub with special soap, Eve.
Brush your teeth, Eve.
Don't swallow any water, Eve."

Worried that if I didn't
announce the next move
out loud, I
might not make it.

"Sure you don't need the bathroom
one more time?" my mother
asked, as she turned to

lock the door.
I shuddered.
Out of all the physical horrors
leading up to this day,
the enema had been
by far
the worst.
You'd think they would have figured out
a better way to get
that done.
I was empty. And I
felt empty,
for more reasons than the
graphically violent last few hours
I'd spent in the bathroom.

Because the fact was
whenever I had imagined
this moment in my life,
and I had imagined this moment
many times,
Lidia was with me.

"Got your bag?" my mother asked.
She could see it in my hand,
but I knew she
just needed to say something.

"Yeah."

I could see my breath
on the way to the car, but I didn't
feel the cold. I didn't feel
anything.

I don't remember the drive, parking,
or the walk through the hospital—just the
nurse who checked me in.
Name?
Birthday?
Allergies?
Smoker?

I had smoked.
One time.
At Junlin Yu's party last summer
with Thomas Aquinas.

We'd shared it. First his lips
sucking on it. Then mine. Then
his, again.

"We're cool now, Eve," he'd joked when we'd
finished. And I laughed. Because it felt
true. We were cool.

Later that night, Lidia smelled it on me and asked,
"Did you smoke?" And I'd said
no. Not because she'd care if I'd smoked
but because she'd care that I'd smoked...
without her.

When the nurse
asked if I smoked,
I lied
again.

It wasn't until I was
alone in the room
changing into a soft blue gown that my
chest began to
throb with fear.
Was the nicotine
lingering in my lungs?
Would it affect
the surgery?

A second nurse
brought me to a room,
told me to relax,
have a seat.
I didn't relax, but
I didn't sit.

Instead, I paced the
little room, knocking into
plugs and wires and
plastic medical devices. Like I'd lost
all sense of spatial judgment, like I couldn't
be sure I was actually
there.

The room seemed to be shrinking, the walls
closed in around me,
and I became pretty positive
that the cigarette meant everything.

The door swung open.

"Eve Abbott."
It was Dr. Sowah, followed by a
crowd dressed in scrubs.

"I smoked a cigarette last summer,"
I blurted.

He chuckled.
He was always chuckling.
It slowed my heart rate,
his chuckling.
"Ready?" he asked.

I didn't answer.
My arm felt warm.
Then my face.
The room began to retreat
into my eyes.

"You are going to get
sleepy," said a voice,
but I was already
sleepy. And moving.
My mother. In a hall.
Cold.
So cold. Though
Lidia is there
holding me. Under the bright
lights. It hadn't happened yet.
None of it had happened yet.

The Real One

You hugged me
too long.
I let you.
Both of us ignoring the mob of
New Year's Day shoppers
streaming by.

When you finally pulled back,
your face was a blur. Like
the blood pumping through my head
was pumping it past my eyes.

"Bathing suit shopping,"
you said.

"No, Lid."

"Yes! A bikini. It's what you've
always wanted."

"Lidia."
I couldn't move.
I couldn't make myself move.

"Come on, Eve," you begged.
I was about to give in when
he came out of nowhere. Jumping
between us, and making the joke that
you looked tough, and
that I should listen.
He was talking to me.
But he was looking at you.

Of course, his true joke was
that you didn't look tough—
your slender body
lost in the oversize hoodie.
But the joke was on him, because you
were tough. You'd always been
tough.

Just as you were about to give him
the classic Lidia cold shoulder—a
practiced move used on the ever-growing
number of flirting outsiders—he noticed
the fedora.

"May I?" he asked.

Caught off guard,
you nodded.

Gently, he lifted the hat from your head and
placed it at an angle on his own,
posing with
a grin.

A grin that moved both his cheeks
far to the sides of his face and wrinkled his brow.
A grin that held nothing back.

You stood
staring at that grin,
static electricity floating
strands of your long dark hair toward
the atrium of the mall.
"Keep it," you said.

He looked straight into your eyes,
that grin still
solidly in place, and
suggested he borrow it.
"Until next Saturday."

It was a date.
He was making a date with you.

And you
said yes.

His name was Jayden.
Jayden of the grin. And
Jayden of the grin had a friend.
Nick.

Though neither Jayden nor you
asked if this was something
I'd agree to.

Maybe—seeing me twisted and braced, he
assumed I'd agree. Because
what other options did I have?

Whatever he thought—you made the date.
For the movies.
For the both of us.

"Lidia," I said, the second
he was gone. Instantly,
pissing you off.

Lidia.
Just your name.
But what you assumed
I'd meant by it
was apparent.

You just made a date
with someone who does not know
you have one hand.

And yes,
I admit it.
I did mean this.
But I also meant

You just made me a date
with someone who does not know
I'm twisted as fuck.

The Human Form

CAREFULLY, SO CAREFULLY, I PUSH DOWN ON THE KNIFE. The white pill underneath divides in two with a click... and a bit of fine dust, which I press my finger into and stick in my mouth before I set up the next one.

"It's a good plan," she says. "And now when your physical therapist comes, you can tell her you're down to half your regular dose."

"Exactly, Lid!" I cry.

It *is* a good plan, cutting my Roxy in half, doubling my stash, regardless of the fact that it's my *only* plan. For right now, it makes me feel better.

I position the knife's blade in the little nook of another Roxy and apply gentle pressure. The clink of steel meeting the wood of the cutting board is so satisfying—the single pill springing apart into two neat little pieces is like the art of collage, dismantling something old to create something new.

"When I'm done," I tell her, "I'm going to stick all the halves into a plastic baggie and hide it. I'll keep the ones in the bottles whole so my mother doesn't find out." The thought of all my Roxy neatly packaged in plastic and tucked away into a warm space makes me happy. It reminds me of myself.

"Watch what you're doing," she says.

I've cut the pill wrong and it crumbles.

"That's okay," I say, popping the crumbled pieces into my mouth. "I'm allowed to swallow these parts. That's the rule."

"There are rules?"

"Of course there are rules," I say.

"Who makes them?"

I just smile, and she laughs. Because I make them. Although the need to follow them is strangely unaffected by this fact.

When I'm finished, I count the pill pieces. Twice.

"You do know that the amount is actually the same as before you cut them up?" she asks. "Don't you?"

"I do."

But I don't.

Everything we think, everything we know, can change. There is no actual. No literal. No real.

This is the Roxy dust talking.

I count them one last time.

"I'm glad you're not mad at me anymore, Lid," I tell her.

"Why would I be mad at you?"

I pop a wobbly-looking half into my mouth instead of answering and enjoy the scrape of it as I swallow.

I love my Roxy.

———————

Last night I googled how painkillers work. I wanted in on the chunky white pill's journey, to know what happened to it after it passed my lips.

Our bodies are filled with nerve endings. When cells are injured or damaged, they release certain chemicals. When these chemicals hit the nerve endings, the nerve endings respond by whispering to one another—nerve to nerve to nerve—until the message reaches your brain: *You are in pain, a lot of pain!*

But then comes the Roxy.

Sometimes just staring at the bottle makes me happy. It's like I feel dry without it. And I want to feel wet. I can't explain it any better than that.

In fact, I can feel it already, doing the simple little job of wedging itself between the nerves so they can't speak to one another.

No message. No pain.

Proving that it's better not to know.

———————

After hiding my pills in a secret place, I lie down on the couch. Where has Lidia gone? My laptop is sitting on the coffee table. I open Netflix. But the screen with all its colorful choices immediately defeats me, and I close it up and slide it to the floor.

I hate the middle of the day.

And now I hate that I cut up all my Roxy—it made me okay, doing something for a moment, but that translates into not okay in all the other moments.

I turn to face him—the Roxy bits and dust from my work now wedged in all the right places. The sun is shining off his aperture, *aperture* being a fancy name for the telescope's front eye.

Aperture.

"Why are you a telescope?"

"Would you like me to be in some other form?" he asks.

"Some other form?" I say, letting my eyes flutter shut. "Like a giant plastic hamburger?" I need to rest. My apertures. Rest.

I'm almost gone, returning to the quiet, soft place where the Roxy takes me, when I hear him.

"What about the human form?"

Hmmm . . . so not a plastic hamburger?

The Happiest of Huts

Our first day of our first job
we found ourselves
in a smelly locker room
with two giant costumes.

I wanted to be the french fry,
with its spongy, yellow softness
and cool beret.

The hamburger
wore a goofy tuxedo
size Men's XL, and
worse,
it had a huge plastic head.

Huge.

But the french fry had
two puffy yellow hands
built
right into the costume

and the hamburger wore black gloves and
used a cane.

I became the hamburger.

They sent us everywhere . . .
new-building openings,
food festivals, a
medieval fair.

We never spoke.
Food doesn't speak.
We just showed up
and were a hit.
Everywhere.
Even at the medieval fair,
where we competed
with swords and pirate hats.

Lidia said
she loved the
paychecks,
although it was obvious
every time she removed the french fry head—
her hair a frizzy
humid mess,
her face flushed, her
eyes lit like high beams

that it
meant much more than
money.

It was fun.

I loved it.
I loved all of it.
The dirty van and shaggy drivers, who
drove us over potholed two-lane
highways to strange venues
with long tables, gritty floors, and
paper cups filled with sugary juice,
where kids screamed the
second they saw us.
I loved our choreographed dances
set to some mother's idea
of a cool song on her Spotify.
Although calling anything we did
in those giant costumes *dance*
was pushing it.
I even loved the taste of plastic mixed with
my own sweaty breath inside the huge head.
Though I especially loved
the view—looking out through the grinning teeth
of a hamburger.
People stared at me,
as they always did,

but with a straight-on smile instead of
side-eye curiosity.

Acknowledgment.
Approval.
Acceptance.

I hadn't seemed to make
a good human, but
as a hamburger,
I was beloved.

Minnesota

MY MOTHER WAKES ME FROM A SOUND SLEEP. SHE WANTS to talk. I tell her I'm listening, but I'm not...until she says that word.

"...Minnesota?"

I'm listening now.

I logroll off the couch and climb to my feet from my knees with a pretty loud moan.

"You're leaving me alone for two weeks?"

"I'm not leaving you alone, Eve. You'll stay with Mary Fay."

"What? I can't even stay here in my own home?"

"Eve, it's an honor to attend the Minneapolis Poetry Society's retreat and conference. You know I've been applying to it for years. This is the first time I've gotten beyond their wait list. You have to understand—"

"I don't have to understand," I say, cutting her off.

"When you're healing from major surgery you want your own bed."

My mother sighs. "You sleep on that couch half the time."

Is this true? I want to fight her on it.

"And your mother. You want your mother," I add, laying it on pretty thick. "Don't go," I whisper.

She's standing and looking at me. I hate when she does that—looks but doesn't say anything.

Maybe...maybe she's changing her mind. Maybe she sees how wrong it is to leave your suffering daughter for a work thing. Maybe she'll stay.

"I'll ask Meef to come here, okay?" she says, using my nickname for Mary Fay like this makes it better, like she's conceding. And then she turns and heads off into the kitchen.

Her back. Always her back. Walking away, hunched over a desk, a book, her computer. Intent on everything but me.

"What about school?" I shout after her, and instantly regret it. The thought of school sends a shot of fear through me.

"You have almost a week before you go back. And paratransit can get you there. It's probably a lot more comfortable than any car would be for you right now anyway," she says, walking into the kitchen.

School. In less than a week. But that's not tomorrow, or the next day. Or the day after that.

"And Eve," she shouts, interrupting my attempt to morph a week into forever. "Mary Fay is great with sick people because of her mom's multiple sclerosis, and she does a lot of her work from home, so you won't be alone like you are now."

"I'm not sick and I like being alone," I holler, my loud voice sending pain up my spine and through my mangled rib cage.

She ignores me.

"MOM!"

Still no answer.

I pick up my Roxy, yet instead of opening it, I hold the bottle against my chest and turn toward the big picture window. The sky is a bright gray. It looks like it might snow. Or maybe it's just evening.

Dropping to my knees, I roll back onto the couch with the Roxy in my hands and close my eyes. Shutting out everything.

Did I want this? For her to go?

I don't. I know I don't.

Cold. Lakes. Snow.

My thumb rubs along the ridged edge of the plastic bottle top.

Don't open it.

I hear my mother walk back into the room. I hear her sip her wine. It must be evening.

"Mary Fay will have Dr. Sowah's number," she says. And then I guess since she sees me lying there holding my Roxy like a warm little kitten, she adds, "As well as a list of your prescriptions. I just spoke with her and she said it's no problem at all for her to stay here. She'll drive over after dinner on Sunday."

I keep my eyes closed. "Of course Mary Fay said she'd come. She is a caring, loving human."

My mother quickly gets my meaning.

"Eve, stop acting like I'm abandoning you. I've been here every day for six weeks. I'll be here for two more days, and then back before you know it. For god's sake, this is important to me."

I squeeze my eyes shut even tighter. *I'm not important to her. I want to fucking be important to her.*

"Eve."

"I don't need Mary Fay. I'm sixteen, not six."

"As you have just pointed out, you've undergone major surgery. I'm not leaving you alone."

"You leave me alone every single day!"

She winces. "That's different. I'm just a few miles away. And every time you call, I pick up immediately."

I've only called twice, which she knows.

"I'd be fine by myself."

"Blood clots, infection, confusion, nausea, atrophy, atelectasis," she says. "Should I keep going?"

"I don't know what you're talking about."

"Yes, you do," she says.

"Well, I don't know what atelectasis is," I grumble, turning to face the back of the couch.

"It's a collapsed lung. And it can happen after serious surgeries. All those things can happen after serious surgeries. That is why I'm not leaving you alone."

I take a breath.

And then another.

My lungs feel fine? I think? I didn't even know they could collapse.

My mother reads the silence. "Your lungs aren't going to collapse," she says.

I turn my head to face her. "Then why can't I just stay here alone?"

I don't want to stay alone. But I don't know what to say that will keep her here.

She flaps her hands at her sides in frustration and turns around and walks out of the living room. So I guess it wasn't *that*.

"Did you ever think," she says, her voice muffled by the fact that she is walking away from me, again, "that maybe I want to go and do this very important thing in my life without having to worry about you?"

Her words suck the air right out of my perfectly fine lungs, and before I can stop myself, I roar, "I didn't know that you ever worried about me."

My head spins with the emotion of letting those words out into the world.

She stops. She's angry. I can feel it. How dare she be angry. But she doesn't turn around.

Come back. Don't go.

She goes. Leaving me alone.

Except for my Roxy.

Mirrors and Miracles

It's been sixteen hours without Roxy.

That's the new deal. No Roxy and my mother stays safe. The telescope can go fuck himself.

It's also been sixteen hours without sleep. I'm exhausted and I ache from my split ends down to my scuzzy toenails. The only way I can deal with the pain is to lie very still and moan. I'm back in my bedroom with my telescope. I wish he wasn't in here, but I can't ask her to take him out because I love that she moved him without my asking.

I turn my head and look at him. Dust lies on the top of the black cylinder like the first few flakes of snow on the top of a mailbox. His aperture faces the floor. Maybe he's not here anymore.

He is not a he; it is a telescope. A thing. A made-up thing. He was never here.

I take another big breath to test my lungs. They're

working, but greedy-ish, like they need extra air. I pick up my Roxy and shake it. It sounds like a festive little maraca.

I do not need one. My spine throbs, my staples itch, and the tips of my missing ribs vibrate in fear at even my mind approaching them.

But.

I do not need one.

I shake my Roxy again. I remove the top and look at them. My mother will be gone for two weeks. That's a long conference.

Two weeks.

I twist the top back on with a heavy sigh, put the bottle onto my bedside table, and then glance over at him.

I can help you, Eve. But each time I do... a tiny piece of Minnesota will disappear.

I should take my Roxy. My fucking back hurts. I'm in pain. Do I really believe that I made a pact with the devil? I don't. I do not believe this.

But I do. I do believe it.

Frustrated, I close my eyes to get away from him. Yet he somehow feels more present this way. I need to get out of this room.

Rolling off the bed, I head for the bathroom, grabbing my Roxy. It's as if there is some invisible rope that ties us together.

I lock the bathroom door behind me and lean against the tiled wall, soaking up the safe feel of the small room. The light is off, and the gray morning makes my reflection glow white in the full-length mirror. I've always been one of those really white, white girls, but this morning, I look like a blank Word document.

I put down the plastic bottle and stand up off the wall in front of the mirror. I've stood in front of so many mirrors.

So many mirrors.

Although right now I am reminded of only one. Full-length. On the door outside the event trailer bathroom. Where Lidia stood—her french fry head off, staring at herself with two hands.

That imperfect mirror is all in your head.

Such bullshit.

I slipped out before she caught me. It felt wrong, seeing her wanting something she couldn't have.

And here I stand. In front of yet another mirror. Like I've done so many times.

Did I finally have it?

The something I wanted?

Like all those other times, I do not notice anything about myself but the shape of me, wrapped in familiar plastic.

My hands run down either side of my brace.

Nineteen degrees.

Down from seventy-eight.

The sound of the Velcro strap echoes off the tile of the tiny bathroom. My heart speeds up, telling me that I need to slow down. I quickly pull the brace back into place.

I suck in a breath and rip open the Velcro again.

Nineteen degrees.

I let the brace fall and stare at myself in the mirror in my filthy body sock and sweats.

Not crooked. Not leaning. No humps or bumps or bones poking wrong.

Symmetrical.

Linear.

Even.

Shoulders running across in a line. Breasts where one does not sag lower. Hips that follow shoulders. A waist with twin curves. Vertebrae that tell a single tale, all together. The indent of a belly button surrounded by a perfect circle of proportion.

And all of this ease, it glides...silent, tippy, tippy-toe silent brushing past like a pretty skirt against legs.

This is me.

Me!

Me straight.

Me fixed.

And god, I look good.

I look good, and it's what I wanted. To look good.

Then why does it feel wrong to look like this?

Wrong to like it?

You could be straight if you wanted.

———

Grabbing my Roxy, I open up the bottle and...stop. I want to pop one in before I can have any thoughts against it. But I have a thought. Of her in Minnesota. And now I can't.

I lean over the sink and scoop handfuls of cold water onto my face, into my mouth. I wipe my face on a towel and ease down onto the toilet seat.

The four walls snuggle around me, closing me in, and all I see is the white porcelain. The shine of the drain. The light from the window. The tub. The showerhead. The dull blue shampoo bottle. An old razor. I need my life to be as small as this bathroom.

I imagine warm water on my skin. I'm dying to feel it. I'll settle for just listening to it run.

Kneeling, I stop up the tub and start the hot water, watching it swirl over the bath mat. It's so beautiful. My fingertips skim the top of it like skeeter bugs on a pond.

Maybe I can just sit in a couple of inches of it.

I stand up and unlock the bathroom door. My mother is the last person I want to see right now, but I'm not about to have the fire department breaking down my door if I fall and can't get up.

Warm steam fills the bathroom. I pick up the orange bottle and move it to the back of the toilet so it won't fall into the water. It feels nice just touching it.

When the water reaches about two inches, I turn off the faucet. Then I stand up and let my sweats slide to my ankles. The body sock is harder. It takes a ton of wiggling and heavy breathing to pull my arms out and scooch it down over my hips.

Of course I consider looking in the mirror at my totally naked self, but the roller coaster ride my stomach takes just thinking about it has me turn back to my first order of business—the tub. Very, very slowly, I step over the side and put my right foot in the water.

Oh, wow.

Water.

I let the amazing warmth of it soak up through my sole, the heat creeping into my ankle, up my calf. Every muscle in my body screams to be in that tub.

I stay like this for a few minutes, skin tingling, while I gather my wits about me for the next step. It's a big one. I look around for a way to get into the tub where I don't have to lift my second foot from the ground.

There isn't one.

I reach out and clutch the porcelain soap dish tiled into the wall, but it's too slippery.

The only way to do this is by holding on to the shower head.

It's kind of jiggly, though I think it can bear my weight. Holding my breath, I bring my left leg up and over the tub wall and into the water.

"Yesssss," I hiss joyfully.

I'm in.

I carefully lower my rodlike body into the tub—aware of every screw and staple—until I'm sitting on my feet, a circle of warm water around my thighs.

Water is amazing. It really is. Even this tiny amount

makes my now-even shoulders fall away from my ears and allows my lungs to open like two butterflies lifting off into the sky. And, I guess, it turns me into a bad poet.

I yawn so big my jaw cracks.

A very tired poet.

I sit in the tub and stare down at the bath mat. Happy?

Happy.

I hear Sowah's voice.

Nineteen degrees.

A miracle.

Something We Both Knew

On some long-ago
gloomy afternoon
my mother stepped
into my room
with clean sheets. A
simple, neatly folded stack of
clean sheets.

The fitted sheet is kind of fun to put on, but
the flat one sucks. You can
fling it up and out a
hundred times yet
it never lands right.

With zero hope of success, I
picked it up at one end and
flung it into the air with a hefty

snap!

A snap that caught my attention.
A snap that felt right on.

A snap I watched float down to the bed and . . .
land perfectly.

In that moment
a dream was born.
A living, breathing
dream.

The snap.
The floating
down,
down,
down
and the
landing, softly . . .
even.
It is Dr.
Sowah,
holding on to my toes
while I lie
so still,
and then, just like the sheet,
he snaps me
up into the air
     where one by one by
     one,
     the vertebrae in my very crooked spine
     crack,

crack,
crack
into a perfect bumpy line
as I float to the bed
straight at last.

Like all daydreams,
it was satisfying, comforting,
and I spent hours
envisioning this lovely, simple
snap. Ignoring things like
pedicle screws, interbody fusion,
blood.
Just as Lidia
spent hours on her
website, repeating words like
elegant, flexible,
lightweight. Ignoring words like
glove, individual digits, and
TrueFinish™ *technology*.

It was a dream.
There was
no soft landing. And
copyrighting a word like
TrueFinish™
didn't make it true.

But there was a landing.
For me.

You could be straight,
if you wanted.

    Sawed open.
    Rearranged.
    Stapled shut.
    Something we
            both knew.

The Real One

You said
it was his grin.
But I knew
it was my surgery.

The rest of New Year's Day
you spent talking about
that grin...
his bright eyes...
the sure way he'd plucked the hat from your head...
then the grin...
again.

The guy was
literally in our presence
for thirty seconds, yet
somehow,
you'd noticed enough
about him
to pontificate endlessly.

Meanwhile. I didn't say a word—
about what you hadn't told Jayden, or

the dread I felt
imagining Nick's disappointment
when he showed up on Saturday
and found
me.

But what could I have said?
I needed you, Lid.
God, I needed you.
More than I ever had.
Everything was changing.
Literally,
everything.

In two weeks,
my skin,
my muscles,
my bones,
even my belly button
wouldn't be in the same place.

So I did what I'd always done.
I pulled my head inside my plastic shell
and stayed there.

The date was a week away.
Anything could happen in a week.
Holiday break was over.

School started tomorrow.
You'd have volleyball.
Our English term papers.
Your hand on its way.
My surgery around the corner.
You'd forget that grin.
Forget his bright eyes.
You'd forget the date.

Slow Motion

Loud knocking.

My mother.

"Eve!"

The world spins in a tiny circle as I remember where I am.

The bathroom door opens a crack. And then it swings wide.

"Are you in the tub? What the hell, Eve? How did you get in there?"

But she stops and looks away when she sees me hug myself for privacy. She didn't come in here to get angry. She takes a breath and resets herself.

"Hey, how about this," she says. "Let's put some soap in there with you. It looks like you've got a few inches or so before the water reaches the bottom incision. At least you can clean your legs and your...your..."

"What kind of feminist are you that you can't say *vagina*, Mom?" But I'm smiling.

She snorts. "It's actually a vulva," she says.

"Mom." I roll my eyes and drop my arms, modesty over, while she pours bodywash into the water and swishes it gently with her hands to make bubbles, eyeing my staples. It's hard not to notice them. They begin up under my left armpit, run down to my navel, and then over to my right hip. There is a separate track that runs from between my scapula down to my butt. I can't see those. I can only feel them.

"Wow," she says.

I think it's the first time she's seen what Dr. Sowah did. I'm happy to shock her. I sometimes feel so damn…uninteresting to her.

"Hey, I know," she says. "Do you want me to shave your legs? And after I help you out of there, we have you lean over the tub wall and I'll use the shower attachment to wash your hair."

"Um." I think. "I like the shaving-of-the-legs thing, but I'm not sure about the leaning part."

"Well, let's start and see where we get," she says.

She helps me stand and then carefully wraps my many staples up in a towel. This way, I can lean against the shower tiles while she shaves my legs, rinsing off the soap with the shower attachment. The warm water feels so good. The sudden need to be clean is overwhelming.

"Okay, get me out," I say. "Let's try the leaning thing." It's not as good as a real shower, but it's something.

Getting out with my mother's help is so much easier, and so much less scary, than getting in had been. She dries my legs with another towel and then trots off to my bedroom for a clean body sock and a fresh pair of sweats, leaving me alone with the Roxy. I can see it in my peripheral vision but don't move to look directly at it.

When my mother returns, she also has a glass of water. "Where's your medicine?" she asks. "This is a lot of activity for you. You might want to take one."

Stunned, I stare at her. What do I do?

"Eve? Sweetheart?"

Sweetheart.

I point at the Roxy sitting on the back of the toilet.

She picks it up and spills one out, handing it to me. I take it from her in slow motion, bringing the white pill to my lips, moving for the glass, filling my mouth with water. Doing it all because it comes from her. But it's my decision to swallow.

She removes the glass of water from my hand and sets it on the sink counter, and then helps me into the body sock by placing it over my head and carefully rolling it down over my incisions.

I can feel it already. The Roxy. Rushing into all my nooks and crannies like heavy rainwater racing down muddy slopes and bubbling over worn rocks, making its way to a river, an ocean.

I hold on to her shoulders while she pulls on my sweats. The clean cotton sliding up my freshly shaved legs feels so good I shiver.

We Velcro me back into my second home, and then my mother prepares for the hair washing by placing a thick towel on the tub wall for support. I get down on my knees, lean into the tub—belly to towel—and allow my head to hang from my neck. The tug on my sore spine feels strange, but not bad.

"Here goes," she says.

Staring down at the bath mat on the tub floor, I zone in and out while my mother washes my hair, the Roxy sending all my thoughts to a galaxy far, far away. She very delicately douses my head with warm water, lathers my hair using her strong fingers, and gently rinses it while water runs down my face, dripping off my nose, my eyelashes.

"How you doing?" she asks every few minutes.

My only response is "Mmmm."

When she's done, she asks if I can stand it a little longer while she conditions it. I can't. My spine is so done in this position, even with the Roxy.

She towels my wet hair and we go out to the living room where I lie on the couch and she combs my hair out over the armrest. The soft tugging at my scalp puts me into a deep coma-like state where I'm safe and happy and peering out between the branches of yellow forsythia.

"Eve," she says.

My name. The name she gave me. I don't often hear her say it like this. Like she is going to say something that's just for me.

"I'm sorry that I have to leave you."

She's sorry.
Sorry. To leave me.
She's leaving.

Turning from the
mirror . . . toward the
restroom door.

"Lidia, no," I whisper.
   "Eve?"

When I open my eyes, I find my mother standing in front of me.
   I clear my throat. "I think I need more medicine."
   She quickly fetches my Roxy and hands me one. This time, nothing happens in slow motion.
   I watch her turn and walk away.

Alone.
In the living room.
I remember the rumble of the truck,
the squeak of the brakes, and
my signature on the tablet.

The Real One

You didn't forget.

We sat in my living room
over the next week
waiting for the hand, while you
jabbered on and on
about Jayden...
A guy who
basically
stole your hat.

I knew you were attempting to drive
all the things I knew,
all the things you knew,
out of our minds as we munched on veggie sticks,
twisted our hair into different romantic messy buns,
and
watched out the window for the UPS truck.

You never brought up my surgery, but
neither did I. Ten days and getting closer every second.
So was Saturday, which was coming even faster.

You were seriously busy.
Trying on everything in your closet.
Trying on everything in mine.
Each outfit chosen to show off your coming
hand.
Your coming hand.

As Saturday approached, I could feel what
little control I had
slipping away.
Still. I tried.
"Lid—" I said,
that Friday afternoon
as you lined your eye
in smoky grays.

"Don't," you said,
cutting me off so fast and final
it left me breathless and
struggling under the weight of
every single moment in my life
where I'd felt
different and
awkward and
ugly and
deformed and
wrong,
just fucking wrong.

You showed up Saturday night
with your eyelashes
dark and long, and your
cheeks flushed red with
Tea Rose Tickle
blush.

You did not wear a hat, but you
did wear a dress.
One with long, flowing sleeves.
You were gorgeous.

"Fuck the hand,"
you said, and we
hopped in your car, and
drove off.

Fuck the hand.
You didn't need it.
Fuck the hand.
You could do anything.
Fuck the hand.
You never needed two hands.
Fuck the hand.
The one you weren't hiding
under your sleeve.
Because I had it hidden
under my bed.

Say Something

"Honey, I'm home!" Mary Fay shouts, startling the shit out of me on the couch, which sends pain shooting everywhere. I groan, but Mary Fay misses it under the clatter of her suitcase rolling across the threshold.

My mother rushes out of her bedroom, greeting Mary Fay with a big hug and kiss. Even Mary Fay is a little knocked off-balance by it. It's strange to see my mother being so affectionate. She's obviously excited to leave.

She's leaving.

I can't help glancing guiltily at my orange bottle.

"More in the car?"

"A bit," Meef says.

My mother disappears out the front door while Mary Fay drops a heavy-looking shopping bag onto the nearest armchair, rolling her suitcase into the center of the living room. "How's the patient?"

It's more a greeting than a question, and she heads back out to help my mother unload the rest of her stuff.

Alone again, I close my eyes and fade away. Although now it's my mother's turn to clop across the threshold and I can't help but crack open my eyes in pure annoyance. Mary Fay is right behind her rolling a second suitcase even louder than the first.

"In the bedroom?" my mother asks, struggling under the weight of two shopping bags' worth of books.

"No, maybe on the dining room table," Meef says, grabbing one from her and dumping it on the table. "This all yours?" she asks me, gesturing toward my stack of homework. I blink at her, hoping that like her greeting, this question also doesn't need a response.

Mary Fay picks up my history textbook and smiles over the top of it. "Me and Eve. Drinking the java and burning up our brains."

"I can't wait," I say. Feeling very much like I can wait. A long time, in fact. And also, that maybe I'm in some trouble.

"Okay, let's get you settled in," my mother suggests.

Mary Fay places my textbook back onto the table and heads for one of the suitcases, while my mother takes hold of the other.

"Nice telescope," Mary Fay says, before they head down the hall past my bedroom to my mother's.

I close my eyes. My telescope is a sore subject at the moment.

"What's it doing in the middle of the living room?" I hear her ask.

"She likes to be with it," my mother says.

"Why?"

"Um." My mother falters.

I lift my head off the couch...waiting to hear how she'll respond to this. "I don't know," she says finally, with a laugh.

It was a piece of the truth. She *didn't* know. The other piece, of course, was *why* she didn't know.

They continue to chat and laugh and generally bump about as they unpack Mary Fay. Where is my silent house? The quiet I'm used to. Hearing them heading back my way, and realizing escape is necessary, I roll off the couch onto my hands and knees, and then stand up way too fast.

Dizzy...my eyes circling in my head...is when I see him.

Thomas Aquinas. Standing in the front door like he is another of Mary Fay's suitcases.

I stop and blink.

"Hey, Eve. Didn't mean to startle you."

He's carrying my trig textbook with a bunch of papers stuck in it.

"I knocked, but—"

"No problema," my mother says from behind me, waving him inside.

"Mom, don't."

She doesn't look at me but stops her terrible Spanish. "Thomas, you've met my partner, Dr. Walker. Mary Fay, you remember Eve's friend Thomas. He lives down the street and has been kindly ferrying Eve's schoolwork back and forth."

"A little more forth than back." Thomas smiles broadly... at me.

"Of course, of course," Mary Fay says. "Thomas. It's good to know I've got help with Eve for the next two weeks."

When she turns her attention my way, Thomas mouths the word *friends* and gestures at the two of us, smiling.

Since I don't understand exactly how to take it, because it is Thomas Aquinas we're talking about, I snap back: "I don't need any help." Trying hard not to look so helpless hobbling back toward the couch, grimacing as I sink onto it.

"Are you in pain?" Mary Fay asks. "Can I get you anything? Your medicine? A glass of water?"

Mary Fay grabs a blanket from the armchair and heads toward me.

"I guess I could use a glass of water?" I shrug as she covers me gently with the blanket.

"I thought you didn't need any help," Thomas says.

When I look over at him, he raises his annoyingly thick eyebrows a centimeter higher.

He is such an asshole.

"That's true," I say, now feeling like I have an illegal blanket covering me.

There is no way to miss Thomas's eye roll, unless you're Mary Fay or my mother. "Why don't I get you a glass of water," he says, turning toward the hallway and our bedrooms.

"Kitchen's to the left," I call out weakly, fiddling with

the blanket to avoid looking directly at Mary Fay's concerned face.

My mother walks into the living room rolling her suitcase behind her just as Thomas walks in and hands me my glass of water. "Eve doesn't have to be waited on," she tells him.

Thomas smirks. I ignore him and take a sip of water.

Mary Fay puts on her coat.

"You don't have to take me to the airport," my mother says. "I'll get a Lyft."

"Nonsense," Mary Fay says, waving my mother's suggestion aside. "How often do you head out to speak at your first big conference?" And then she gestures over at me. "Unless you don't want Eve alone."

"No, no, Eve is fine alone."

I nod in agreement.

"It's just that you've already come all the way out here."

But now I don't know what to do with my head when my mother mentions Mary Fay's sacrifice in taking care of me.

"It'll only take forty minutes. Thomas, do you mind hanging out until I get back?"

"No!" Both Thomas and I say it at the same time.

"Great," Mary Fay says, not knowing how else to respond to our little chorus.

My mother reminds me to brush my hair and teeth as per Nancy's instructions, making me feel like I'm four years old—and even younger when she kisses her hand and plants it on my forehead to say goodbye. The whole thing is made worse by Thomas standing ten feet away.

They head toward the door when my mother stops. "I almost forgot." She expertly picks up my telescope and whisks it down the hall to my room. She's back before I can get too uncomfortable trying not to make eye contact with Mary Fay or Thomas. "Good luck with school, honey," she says.

My heart flutters. "Wait!" I shout.

Startled, my mother stops short in the doorway.

I don't look up, yet I can completely feel Mary Fay and Thomas staring at me. Oh my god, I'm a fucking diva now. But she's about to drive away, and, well, I know Minnesota isn't disappearing. But what if it is? I took the Roxy—I've *been* taking it. And I don't know the rules.

"Uh," I say, out of breath. "Thanks, Mom." Tears sting the corners of my eyes, sprung out of shame or fear, I'm not sure which. I totally blame Thomas-fucking-Aquinas.

"Oh, honey," she says. "You're welcome."

I lie back on the couch, exhausted from the exchange, and after an awkward second, Mary Fay grabs her car keys and ushers my mother out ahead of her, calling back a "see you soon" and shutting the door behind them.

Did I think saying something would keep her here? No. I didn't. I took the Roxy. Just like I took the hand.

I knew she'd go.

Who You Want Me to Be

It's now just me and Thomas Aquinas.

"Um," I say. "I should go to bed."

I pull off Mary Fay's blanket.

Thomas moves uneasily, as if to help me from the couch.

"I got it," I tell him.

I don't feel so snarky anymore. I guess he doesn't either.

He takes his time choosing a seat so as not to watch me logroll off the couch, finally settling into the gold armchair. I'm immediately reminded of Lidia in that very same chair. And I'm dizzy from the strangeness of it. That he is here. That she is not.

"You don't have to stay," I blurt. "I'm fine."

"It's no problema," he jokes.

Seeing me cringe, he adds, "Truthfully, I really have nowhere else to be."

We look at each other with that sentence hanging

between us, and so instead of just saying good night, I say, "And you're already in the chair."

He smiles, settling with extreme exaggeration into the seat. "I am. Already in the chair."

"Okay, good night then." The words stick a little coming out because it feels too weird to be saying this to him.

"Good night," he says. "I'll be right here, in the chair, if you need me."

I nod super-awkwardly, and then get the hell out of there before anything else ridiculous can leave my mouth.

———

My room is warm, although I shut the door anyway. I even turn out the light, like he might be able to see me through the door. Shuffling over to my bed, I sit down on the edge of my mattress, not knowing exactly how to be with my mother gone and Thomas Aquinas sitting in my living room. Even the walls around me, heavy with my life, seem unfamiliar.

I rustle in my drawer, take out a half, and swallow—I am playing my telescope's game now. I made the pact.

Listening to my heartbeat, I sit, frozen, waiting, waiting, waiting. I can't bring myself to move from the edge of my mattress. To admit to living.

Finally, I move. Take another half. Why not. It's over now. Whatever it is. And I sit staring out into all the universes swirling on my dark walls, my stomach swirling with them. Finally, it comes—the first sense of well-being since Mary Fay and her suitcase clattered through the front door.

Inhaling deeply, I roll onto my bed and pull my sheet and blanket up over the top of me and lie like I'm in a movie, flat on my back with my head squarely in the middle of the pillow and my arms folded over the top of the blanket. My eyes won't close.

Because.

Thomas Aquinas is sitting by himself in my living room.

Although now I think about how Thomas Aquinas is always sitting by himself. In fact, I try to picture him hanging out with someone, anyone. Between class. Walking down the hallway. At lunch. Or even on the street. I can't. He is always by himself. Even now, even on a weekend. Out there. In my living room.

As if he can feel me thinking about him, he clears his throat down the hall and it sends a weird bolt of electricity through me. I nervously glance over at my telescope. My eyes haven't adjusted to the dark and I can barely make it out. It's quiet...empty.

Turning my face back to the ceiling, I listen—wanting to hear him out there. I can feel him thinking about me. It's... nice. I like him thinking about me. I lie in my film-sleeping pose, my hands resting across my chest on my brace, and stare into nothing. Nice. I think.

Nice.

Nice.

Nice. Beats my heart.

Yet I can't remember now
what is nice.
The Roxy pumping
into my fingertips
my knees,
across the top of my head.
Minnesota.
The pact.

It's not like the pact means anything. Minnesota is not
disappearing. I've been checking its wiki page almost every
day between episodes of whatever I'm bingeing, along with
searching its news and weather. Nothing has changed. My
mother is heading out to a state where nothing has changed.
I close my eyes and sigh, long and loud.
"You are not real."
"I'm as real as you make me."

His voice tickles
the back of my neck and
my lips curl into a
very large smile.
I hate him.
So much that I love him.
And oh my god,
I've missed him.
"Eve."

He sounds closer than he ever has before. I keep my eyes closed, afraid he won't continue talking if I open them, and I pull the covers tight.

"Then you're not real."

He laughs, and I can
feel it across
every inch of my skin.

"Words are sounds," he says. "The sound is the meaning, not the words. And I understand yours."

But then I hear her voice,
Fuck the hand.
And I know he's right.
Words are just sounds.
"Who are you?"

Fuck the sadness for pushing its way through the Roxy. Fuck the Roxy for not working hard enough. I should have chewed.

"I already told you," he says.

"The devil?"

"Do you really think there is one god, and his nemesis is a dude with a pitchfork?" he asks.

I think about god . . .

and the many nights I
prayed for him to fix me.

"And did you get what you wanted, Eve? Did Lidia?"

He's never said her name before. I slowly open my eyes.
And there, sitting in my desk chair, is Thomas Aquinas.

I clutch at my covers, pulling them up to my eyes.

"What are you doing in here?"

But then he smiles, and I know.

"You're not Thomas Aquinas."

I can feel my heart thudding against my brace.

"Who are you?" I ask. "Why are you here?"

"I thought we agreed on the human form," he says.

He makes a move to stand.

"No!"

I don't want him to move. I don't want him near me. I
don't want this happening.

He leans back in the chair and folds his arms across his
chest.

"Okay, Eve."

The sound of his voice calms me. It always does.

"Really . . . who are you?"

"I am who you want me to be. It's who I've always been."

Now I'm pissed.

"I don't want you to be anything. I don't wa-want you to
be here." I stutter, because I know it isn't true. I do want him
here. I more than want him here. And he knows it.

I slip down into my bed, trying not to think the words
I need you. Though I feel them. Everywhere. And I quickly
close my eyes to hide it. My need.

    For *him.*
    For something that
    doesn't exist.

    Raspy sobs
    scratch in my ears, and
    my body
    jerks at my staples.

    "Eve?"

    He is near.
    I can feel the warm
    weight of him
    like my brace
    wrapping around me.

<hr>

"Drink," he says. He moves the glass to my mouth. Holding
the straw against my lips. His fingers, rough.
    I drink.
    He takes the glass and sets it on the table, but he doesn't
move away.

"I didn't," I tell him, wiping the mess from my face on my pillow.

"What, Eve? What didn't you?"

"Get what I wanted. I didn't get what I wanted. I don't even know what it was."

My eyes have adjusted to the dark because I can see him clearly. His gold-rimmed glasses. His dark hair falling on his shoulders. He's unshaven, as usual. As usual? And he smells like a clean T-shirt straight from the dryer. All of a sudden, I'm dying to press my face into his chest, to suck in the scent of that shirt. The yellow one. The Minnesota one.

Car tires crunch gravel, and he turns toward the sound, but my eyes stay on the T-shirt.

"You're wearing his shirt."

The Real One

You were hatless.
And the way your eyes
searched the crowd
made you look smaller,
younger.

We stood by the benches
in front of the theater
across from the food court.
We didn't speak.

Who knows what you were
thinking. I only know
I wasn't. The echoing hum of the mall
falling on my ears like
steady rain.
Scared shitless
they'd show.
Scared shitless
they wouldn't.

They showed.

Although it was obvious
by the distant look in Nick's eyes
he was here to endure this
for a friend. I was to be
endured.

Had I hoped
it would be different?
Hell, yes, I had.
I had hoped.
And although he couldn't see my brace
under the large sweater I borrowed from you,
no amount of body positivity could transform
my limp,
my lean,
the hump on my back,
into something
he had hoped to find.

I was crooked as hell.
This mattered, and
although I might imagine a different world,
I didn't live in one.

Jayden—wearing your hat and his grin—
didn't notice the cloud of disappointment
swirling around him. Neither did you.

And as the four of us dangled
at the edge of the food court
clicking and clacking against
one another like wind chimes in a light breeze,
I couldn't stop noticing your sleeve,
your very long sleeve,
and how you twisted that sleeve behind your back.
Nervous.
You were nervous.

Then Jayden reached up,
plucked the hat from his head
and returned it to yours—his hands
lingering near your ears
longer than they needed to.

You held your breath—and
a thought landed in my head
like a little bird
out of nowhere.
A light, fluttery thought.
Maybe it will work out.

A Shower

"EVE!"

I smell bacon.

My stomach rolls. I have absolutely no appetite—actually, I have less than no appetite. Food looks horrible. It smells horrible. The thought of it is horrible. I've been living on dry toast and half glasses of milk for over a month now. My mother didn't give it a second thought. Mary Fay does.

My hand reaches for my orange bottle. Food or Roxy. There isn't room in there for both.

"Eve!"

Oh my god. Eating or dealing with Mary Fay? I take a half. And then sink back onto my pillow.

I'm drifting off to somewhere else . . . my favorite place, his place, when—

"Your eggs are getting cold!"

"Coming!" I shout, feeling the sound vibrate down my spine, although not nearly the way it once did.

Throwing off my covers, I logroll to a sitting position like the tree trunk I am, but then stop, self-conscious when I remember him. Licking my lips, I run my fingers through my hair, as though he might be able to see me right now.

"Eve!" The woman is relentless. "Time to eat. Then it's shower time. Remember the bargain? You get a few more days out of school and I get to breathe inside this apartment without your suffocating stink. It's time to pay the piper."

Fuck the piper. And fuck school. I'd do anything not to go back there. Tightening my brace around the ache in my stomach, I head for the kitchen, giving Mary Fay my best version of a smile.

"Good morning," she says, helping me into the chair in front of a plate of scrambled eggs and bacon with a side of rye toast.

Rye is my favorite. I wish that helped me right now.

I shovel a forkful of eggs into my mouth, hiding my gag just as my stomach growls. The human body is superstrange.

"Hungry?" she asks, leaning back against the kitchen counter, watching.

I shrug, letting the eggs slide down my throat just because I need my throat to breathe. "Have you heard from my mother?"

My question has the desired effect: Mary Fay forgets about food.

"She'll text us soon, Eve. Like I told you, conferences

are funny places. They suck you into them, like some sort of black hole."

I inhale slowly through my nose, trying to settle my stomach. A black hole. I've wished my mother into a black hole. Yet I don't stop taking the Roxy. Because? Because I'm in pain. Because I had a major surgery. Because my doctor prescribed it. Because who knows why.

"Eve?"

I don't answer.

"She loves you, honey."

"I know," I growl. I do know. I do. Although it may be right this second that I'm actually realizing it.

"But...she left."

Mary Fay sighs, hugging the dish towel to her bright pink button-up shirt that looks pretty against her dark skin. "I think that sometimes...your mom gets scared of the responsibility."

"She's afraid of me?"

"She's not afraid of you, Eve. She's afraid of making a mistake."

"A mistake? Like, as in a single one? Because she makes a million of them. You'd think she'd be used to it."

Mary Fay laughs, turning her attention toward wiping down the counters. "I'm here, Eve. And I'm not going anywhere. Now eat your breakfast."

I quickly use the moment to break my bread into pieces and stick it inside my napkin along with an entire strip of bacon. When she turns back, she smiles. I've always liked her smile. It's crooked, like me, with one side of her lips showing more teeth than the other. She's buying my show.

"Wonderful. Finish that up and then it's into the shower," she says, returning to the dishes. "We're also going for an outing to the grocery store."

"What?"

She turns from the sink. "You know what Nancy said."

According to my pain-in-the-ass physical therapist, I wasn't getting out enough. It's something she's been saying for a while—and something Mary Fay heard for the first time yesterday yet takes seriously.

"But I look like shit," I whine. The truth of this depresses me further when I think back to leaving bed a few minutes ago.

"You'll feel better after a shower. According to your surgery paperwork, your incisions were allowed to get wet February twenty-fifth. And it's March second."

I have paperwork? That she read.

"I placed two bath towels on the toilet for you."

It's March?

"Remember Nancy's instructions. Don't close the door all the way. Hold on to the bars. Take. Your. Time. And *call me* if you need anything at all!"

My mother had shower bars installed the afternoon after my bath. It amazes me every time I walk into the bathroom.

"People might be at the store," I try. "You know, people I care about not seeing me."

"It's eleven in the morning on a Tuesday," Mary Fay says. "All the *people* will be at school."

"Some of them get early release and they work at the grocery store," I continue. I don't want a shower or an outing. I'm happy in my room.

"Early release?" she says, turning back around to face me. "That sounds like prison, not school."

Mary Fay had been homeschooled all her life. *Homeschooled! What an excellent idea. I'd never have to go back.*

"Meef?"

"Yes, honey?"

"Will you homeschool me?"

"No."

"Even though my mother left me and I'm sad?"

"No."

I sigh. I'll work on that one later. Right now, I have to eat because she's standing there watching me. I swish my eggs around and stick another bite in my mouth. They taste like warm slime. She swipes my Roxy off the kitchen counter and puts it by my juice. "It's been a while," she says, glancing down at the time on her cell phone.

I open the bottle and break a Roxy in half, swallowing the larger chunk and placing the other back in the bottle.

"I like that you're down to half a pill, Eve."

I don't offer that I already took a half this morning. Or that me taking it may be wiping the woman she loves from the face of the earth. Not that I believe this. I don't believe this. The half Roxy on its way into my bloodstream helps me not believe it even more.

"Okay, my heavy metal friend," she says. "I guess we can

go to the grocery store before you take a shower. Avoiding the *early releasers*."

I am going nowhere like this. I haven't seriously washed in god knows how long. And according to Mary Fay, I stink.

"I'll take a shower and we can go after," I say, standing up from the table.

Mary Fay stops me. "Eve," she says, looking down at my plate. "You didn't eat very much."

I have a missing-my-clueless-mother pang. "I'm never that hungry in the morning, Meef. You know lunch is my big meal."

She nods, and I escape. Yet it's obvious she doesn't believe it.

Wobbling down the hall toward the bathroom, all I want to do is crawl into bed and pull the covers up to my ears. Picturing myself in the grocery store the way I look right now compels me into the bathroom.

Easing the door *almost* closed, I leave the light off and start the shower. I stand, staring at the daylight streaming in through the frosted window and listening to the water, while steam fills the room. The idea of stepping into that water gives me goose bumps.

Mary Fay is out there, clattering about the house. Since the moment she arrived, I've had zero peace.

As if on cue, she yells, "Holler if you need me, sweetie!"

Sighing, I undo my brace, pull off my pajamas, and reach for the new bar while v-e-r-y s-l-o-w-l-y raising my foot up and over the side of the tub. Water hits my leg and I start shivering all over.

I stand there for a few minutes, watching the blur of cars through the window. Finally, I shift my weight to the foot in the tub and bring my other one to meet it, clutching the bar with both hands.

I'm in.

Closing the curtain and letting the shower do what it does—stream out of a hundred holes—I look down at myself. The sun shining in through the shower window glints off the long line of shiny metal staples. My pulse quickens, my head spins. It's too steamy. There isn't enough air.

I rip open the shower curtain and gulp down cool air like it's water, holding tightly to the bar.

After a few minutes, my heartbeat slows and I let my chin fall to my chest, watching the water pool around my feet while steam surrounds me like a warm cloud. Closing the shower curtain again, I ease backward into the water stream.

When it hits my spine, I gasp. The warmth and the weirdness seem to mix together creating some emotional elixir. And I start to cry, as quietly as I can manage, so Mary Fay won't hear.

Although when I finally douse my head with water, I can't contain the loud sob.

"Eve?"

"I'm good," I yell. And then I add, "I'm really good." Because I am.

I grab the shampoo and dump half the bottle on my hair and then lather with the tips of my fingers because it hurts to raise my arms. There are so many bubbles they threaten to drown me.

Oh my god, oh my god, oh my god.

I use the pile of bubbles streaming down my shoulders to wash my body.

Oh my god, oh my god, oh my god.

I imagine this is what the Vikings must have felt like when they returned from some yearlong sea voyage and finally got to bathe—if they'd had grapefruit-lemongrass shampoo. And then I dump another round of it over me and lather again.

Oh my god, oh my god, oh my god.

This is heaven! I don't think about stopping until I hear Mary Fay again. "Eve, it's been a minute, honey."

I turn off the faucet, and it's like the running water is connected to my energy level because suddenly I'm exhausted.

But I'm also freezing.

I make my way out of the tub the same way I made my way in…slowly and thoughtfully. Then I wrap up in both the gigantic towels, pick up my brace, and leave the bathroom.

Mary Fay is hovering in the hall. "You good?"

"Yes," I say, shivering.

"Give me a shout if you need help getting dressed. I'm an expert at dressing others, remember."

I only met Mary Fay's mom once before she died—the

MS had her in a wheelchair by then—but I knew she lived with Mary Fay at the end.

Nodding through chattering teeth, I shut my door.

Sitting down on my bed is probably not a good idea, and an even worse idea all wrapped up in warm towels, yet I can't stop myself.

"Ten minutes, Eve," Mary Fay calls.

I lie back and close my eyes.

Ohhhh . . . lying down brace-less is heaven, the soft towels against my skin, my bones meeting a giving mattress.

"You're going to be in trouble," he whispers.

Now I feel all that skin in another way, imagining what it would be like to be touched by him. I don't dare open my eyes. Afraid he'll be there . . . afraid he won't.

The Real One

You were switched on.
It looked like you could
barely stop yourself from
burrowing your face into his neck and
wrapping yourself around him. I'd
never seen you like this.

He was totally feeling you.
Everything out of his mouth was
suggestive, and you treated
each innuendo like a serve that you
expertly volleyed back into his court.

You didn't include me.
You couldn't. You were
too busy drowning in the frothy joy
of his eyes, all over your eyes,
all over you.

When the four of us
walked into the dark theater,
you tried to steer him into the aisle first, to
position him on your right side. But he was

so gallant, gesturing with his arm,
"After you, m'lady," and
who could resist that?
You couldn't.
So you strode into that aisle,
swaggering to your seat.
Knowing he was staring hard at your ass
and knowing how good it looked.

Did I feel the chilly ache
of your vulnerability?
I did, Lid. I did.
But there they were.
Jayden and Nick.
Separating us like a
warm unfamiliar wall.

The movie started.

It was then that Jayden
must have decided to hold your hand—
a hand he'd never once considered
might not exist.

Forced from the Realm

"OKAY, EVE."

She clicks on the light.

Although I can see the brightness through my closed lids, I don't respond, hoping she will just go away. Hoping everyone will just go away.

"I let you sleep for hours. It is now six o'clock, and we are going to the store."

I'm still in my towels. They're cold and wet. And I suddenly feel very naked.

"I've also made an appointment with Dr. Sowah for tomorrow."

My eyes flip open. "What? Why?"

I struggle to sit, but my head's foggy from sleep and I totally fail. Being brace-less now feels unsafe, and I tighten the cold towel around me, trying not to look completely pathetic under Mary Fay's watchful gaze.

After a few seconds, she folds her arms and leans back on her hip. "I don't know," she says, shaking her head. "You just don't look good to me, honey."

"I'm fine," I say, finally sitting up, hoping that she doesn't notice the wobble of my head.

"You were scheduled to go on Friday anyway, Eve, so what's a few days?"

She turns around and starts opening drawers in my dresser.

"Okay, I'll go tomorrow. Now, can I just sleep?"

"I didn't ask you if you wanted to go. I told you I made an appointment," she says, her nose buried in my dresser drawer.

"Won't this mess up your work schedule or something?"

"Don't you worry about my business, Eve," she says, choosing clothes for me.

"I can do that," I tell her, trying to keep the anger out of my voice.

She tosses sweats, a body sock, and a sweatshirt onto the bed, and then stands there—no crooked smile this time, she's all eyes.

"Okay," I tell her. "I'll get dressed."

"I'll be waiting in the living room," she says, walking out of my room. "With my car keys in my hand." And then she shuts the door.

Sighing, I open the bedside drawer and take out my Roxy. I count them up because this is my ritual now—the number of Roxy has replaced the number of degrees of my curve, my brain forever recalculating the changing number against the days of my life.

I hate this part because counting tells me that I need to close the baggie without taking one.

In a swift motion, I pluck out a half, pop it into my mouth, and swallow it before I can think.

Now that the tiny mental fight is over, I'm glad I took it. The Roxy won. It always does.

Putting clean clothes on a clean body is like some dream I once had. But as I go to take off my towels…I remember him.

I don't turn around. I don't want him to know I'm thinking about him. Is he even in the telescope anymore?

As I remove the towel from my head, my cold, wet hair hits my shoulders and I quickly comb through it with my fingers…the Roxy tingles across my scalp. Outside the window are low, puffy dark clouds against a sliver of a moon. A tiny spit of icy rain taps at the window. It's funny how spring rain can look colder than snow.

I check out the thick pair of sweats, the gray body sock, and the hoodie that Mary Fay chose. She forgot to bring me underwear. It would be too hard to get my feet through the holes anyway, especially now that my hands are so far away from them. She also forgot socks. Nancy brought me some sort of stick that's supposed to help me put those on, but I have no idea where it is. Because I haven't needed to put on socks. Because I don't go out.

"Eve," Mary Fay calls. "Creatures are evolving on this earth faster than you're pulling on a sweatshirt."

This is so ridiculous.

I take off my towel and practically rip my body sock trying to get my feet through as quickly as possible. I've never felt so naked in all my life.

He's not a telescope anymore, he's not a telescope anymore, I repeat, knowing how ridiculous I sound, and trying not to think too hard about what he has become. Who he has become. And the feel of his fingers on my lips.

I drop my sweatpants down as low as I can, and manage to struggle in each foot, one at a time. After catching my breath, I grab my brace without turning around so he can't see my sweaty face. Wrapping it around me, I secure it with the Velcro straps. *Ahh, how good it feels to be back inside.*

"Make it happen," Mary Fay calls, scaring the shit out of me.

I pick up my hoodie and Roxy, grab a pair of socks, and head for the living room.

She's standing at the end of the hall and I can tell she's upset although she's trying not to show it. When I hold out my socks and smile, she sighs.

"Come on. I'll stick them on in the living room."

I'm obviously not getting out of this. Strangely, I don't know how it happened. How I let it happen. Or how I'm going to do it.

A Kiss

EXCEPT FOR A WALK OUT TO THE STREET AND BACK THAT Nancy made me take, I have not left my house since the EMTs rolled me, screaming, into it following the surgery. Mary Fay opens the front door and takes my arm, and I'm screaming as I leave it, although only in my head.

The drive takes less than ten minutes, but the traffic lights and car engines and Mary Fay's foot on the gas and then her foot on the brake and the smell of the car and the smell of the gasoline at the gas station and especially the loudly nightmarish commercials running on the television at the pump have me exhausted by the time Mary Fay cuts the engine at the grocery store.

Really exhausted.

"Let's do this," she says, clapping. Her enthusiasm isn't catching.

She climbs out and closes her door, and the small

moment I have alone is enough for me to retreat into myself, curling up into a ball in the back of my head. The snap of the opening hatch door, along with the clang of Mary Fay removing my forearm crutches, actually stings as it brings me back. And when she slams the hatch shut, all I can think is how much I want my mother. Because I'd be home in my warm bed right now.

Forearm crutches in hand, Mary Fay opens my door. Groaning loudly, I swing my legs from the car one at a time. Attempting everyday-life things—like getting in and out of cars, walking up and down steps, being around things that slam—not only reminds me how absolutely unbendable my body is but how scarily necessary other people are for me to live through a day.

After I have both legs out of the car, Mary Fay hands me my crutches and grabs me securely under one armpit. I summon my body in an are-you-ready kind of way, and together Mary Fay and I stand me up and out in one motion. Once I'm stabilized and balanced, she lets go yet doesn't move from my side.

"You good?"

I frown.

"Come on, Eve. You can do it."

I cannot do this.

Mary Fay reads my thoughts. "Let's get you inside and then I'll come back out for a cart."

The darkness of the parking lot envelops me. I concentrate on the black asphalt in front of my next step. Mary

Fay puts her hand on my shoulder as we near the automatic doors, like she understands how jarring the jerking motion of them opening is going to be. And it is.

We enter.

The place is teeming with movement, made even more overwhelming by the brutal lighting and the onslaught of sound. Mary Fay leaves me clinging to the courtesy desk right inside the front doors while she heads back outside for a cart. In the second it takes her to vanish from view, I'm hyperventilating with panic, too scared to let go of the desk to reach for the plastic baggie filled with Roxy in my coat pocket.

A man hurries past. His paper bag scrapes my arm and the world dims. Before I can recover, a shopping scooter with its fat tires and wire mesh basket zooms by, sucking the breath straight from my lungs. Now I do let go, digging out a full Roxy and popping it into my mouth like the Lifesaver it is.

Metal shopping carts piled with groceries clatter past, dragging bouncy little kids who threaten to leap toward me at any moment. It's as if I'm standing precariously close to the edge of a broiling river with nothing but the hard edge of a desk to keep me from being swept away. I can feel my spine, swollen with pain, and my wounded flesh punctured with staples cringes at the very real danger surrounding it.

I'm about to ask the courtesy desk to call 911, to get me the hell out of here, when Mary Fay rolls up. "Okay, just stay close," she says, all cheery with that crooked smile of hers and I fucking hate every last tooth in her goddamn mouth right now. "Put your left crutch into the cart and hang on here."

Clutching at the bar in the front of the grocery cart with my left hand, I use my forearm crutch with my right. In my mind's eye I see my walker sitting by itself in the corner of my bedroom, a mistake. It would have been much better shelter against the chaotic motion happening in every single aisle. Just imagining one of these carts ramming into my newly solidifying spine makes tears pop into the corners of my eyes every time one rolls near.

Another missing-my-mother moment rises in me while we stand for endless minutes in front of the coffee—my mother and I both walk into a grocery store with one goal, to get what we need and get out. Mary Fay inspects every bag of pasta and box of cereal—not even in an annoyed way, but like she's interested in it. My eyes blur the long shelves of food until it's all a single block of color.

The vitamin section is even worse. We're there so long I'm sure Mary Fay is sprouting gray hairs. Who knew there were so many vitamins? It seems once they ran out of the twenty-six letters in the alphabet, they moved to adding numbers to them like a vitamin bingo game. I sway into the metal shelves, knocking over a row of bottles.

"You all right?" Mary Fay asks, not really looking at me.

"Mm-hmm," I answer, although I don't move off the shelf or right the vitamins.

By the time we get to the baked goods aisle I'm ready to

crawl on top of the loaves of whole wheat bread and sleep for a week.

"All I need is the deli and a few things from the dairy section," Mary Fay announces.

"Can I go sit in the car?" I ask. "I'm so tired."

"Sure. I'll walk you out. Not bad for a first trip back out into the world. You did well, Eve."

Some of my old love of Mary Fay returns in that moment, and when I smile at her it's actually genuine.

"No, I can do it," I tell her, reaching for my second crutch and her keys sitting on top of her purse. "You finish up, Meef."

Where thirty minutes ago I had been petrified of being alone in this place, the Roxy really has me feeling fine. Very fine. As if all I need to do is blink my eyes and I'll be in the car. First, though, I have to hobble out of the bread aisle. Slowly. Deliberately. Because she's watching. Yet as soon as I'm out of her sight, I sloppily clank toward the front doors. Which seem to be moving away from me.

I'm shuffling past a huge display of toilet paper two aisles later when the floor seesaws beneath my feet and my eyesight darkens. Sucking in a sharp breath, I stare out across the long row of checkout counters lined up like lanes at a bowling alley. The world is too 3D . . . people, carts, kids, and it's all happening between me and the exit.

Stopping to catch my breath, I reach out and grab the metal shelf loaded with toilet paper. The car's too far. Way too far. A tsunami of fear breaks over me, making me think I might pee right here on the floor of the grocery store. I need Meef. I need her.

I turn without thinking, without care, and my foot catches on something. I kick it, losing what little balance I had, causing me to swing back into the toilet paper, my crutch clanging against metal. My heart pounds against my brace. A horrible coldness blows through me, gripping my throat.

My lungs are collapsing. I'm going to fall! And my lungs are *collapsing*. It's the atelectasis thing.

I'm going to die in the middle of the Stop & Shop.

Hanging by one hand to the shelf, I'm sweating and panting and freaking out. Somehow I'm also trying hard not to let anyone in the grocery store know that I'm sweating and panting and freaking out. It's embarrassing to be dying like this, in front of all these shoppers. But I can't hide the ugly secret of my impending death because it's happening. It's totally happening.

Frantic, I call out for help.

And he's there.

He grabs my arms and stands me back up. I clutch at the apron strings around his neck, my nose inches from his skin. Again, that fresh T-shirt smell. Why is he wearing a red apron? I look up at him. The lights of the store shine out of the lenses of his gold-rimmed glasses.

"Hang on," he says.

I wrap my arms around him. The human form feels so good.

"Not to me, Eve," he says, "to the shelf."

I don't understand.

He takes my hands from him and puts them onto the shelf. Then he gets down on his knees at my feet. He ties my shoe. When he stands back up, his face is so close to mine. Just like the long line of coffee on the shelf, everything is a blur—the bandanna pulling back his hair, his eyes behind his glasses, his lips. His lips. I lean into them, closing my heavy eyelids. They are warm . . . and still.

I kiss him again.

His lips are so soft in their hesitation, but he does not move away and this just makes me kiss him longer, harder.

He breaks down, kissing me back. Although only for a second before he stops and pulls away.

He's all warm haziness as he leans me back onto the toilet paper and picks up the keys from somewhere on the floor.

"Mary Fay's car?" he mumbles.

I nod yes.

He hands me one of my crutches, keeping the second. Carefully, he shores me up from behind with his arm, gently guiding me through the mess of color and movement to the exit. When the automatic doors open, I don't even flinch. We're hit by a blast of chilly air, and I feel him gently tighten his grip around me.

It must be snowing because tiny freezing specks hit my

cheeks, but his body is so very warm next to mine that the icy wetness feels refreshing.

He opens the door and lowers me in. He places the keys on my lap and when the door shuts, it's like all sound has been erased from the world. My head rests against the cold window and I shiver because of the cold. Because of that kiss.

––––––––––

Mary Fay climbs heavily into the car next to me.

"Hey, Sleeping Beauty."

I'm smiling. I can feel it.

She plucks the keys from my lap and within a second, the engine hums to life beneath me. Heat hits my knees. I slip off into darkness as the car pulls out onto the road.

"Saw your friend in there," she says.

"Friend?" I don't need to hear her say his name; I already know it.

Oh, shit.

The Roxy

I'T'S LIKE EIGHT IN THE FREAKING MORNING AND MARY FAY is crawling us through traffic to Mass General. I haven't recovered from last night's grocery trip and that damn toilet paper kiss. Yet here I am, back in the car.

This woman is killing me.

I woke to the snap of my shade, music blaring from the kitchen, and a stack of clean clothes in her arms, including socks and the sock aid. Although the real cherry on Mary Fay's good-morning cake was a baggie of rye toast for me to eat in the car. "No table service," she'd announced.

By the time we pull into MGH's circular drop-off area, my spine is literally hanging from its rods. I did not allow myself to take any Roxy this morning. At the crack of dawn, it had seemed like a good idea to show up in real and true pain. Not so much anymore, since now I am in real and true pain.

Over the past few weeks, I've been playing the halfsy

game. The hiding-it-away game. The this-isn't-happening game. But the prescription is done. And although I have a supply squirreled away in my bedside table, there are no more refills in my future. I have to ask Dr. Sowah for more. Which does not feel at all like a game.

Mary Fay puts the car in park directly in front of the giant mechanized revolving door. The shred of rye toast crust I nibbled churns in my stomach.

More Roxy. I'll figure out everything else later.

Everything.

My god, I need a Roxy.

"Eve? You okay?"

"Yeah, sorry, Meef. I'm good. You ready?"

She doesn't move.

"You know I'm here for you, honey. Don't you?"

This is not what I need right now. Nodding, I fumble to unbuckle myself. Not that I could get away from her anyway. I'm stuck in this car until she decides to get me out.

"Thanks, yes. I know." I flash a smile, anything to make her move.

It works. Mary Fay returns my smile and exits the car. And I let out the breath I didn't know I'd been holding. She grabs my crutches from the hatchback, and together—like we've been doing this all our lives—we haul me up and out of the car.

She hands over my crutches.

"I only need the one," I tell her. Unlike in the grocery store, I feel safe at MGH. Even with a ton of people around.

She tosses the crutch into the back seat and shuts the door. "I'll park and hang in the waiting room. Text if you need me in with you and the doctor."

"Do you want anything from Starbucks?" I offer, trying to return us to our normal easy conversation.

"Starbucks?" she says. "You need to powershop, Eve. You're already late."

"I'll take that as a no." I'm definitely doing Starbucks.

Turning toward the door, I have a flashback of swaying darkness and pain from the night they stuffed me in an ambulance to take me home. It seems like years ago, not weeks.

My phone vibrates with a text. Mary Fay must want coffee after all.

Wish I could be there with you. *My mother.* Who has not disappeared. Who is at a conference in a state that is not disappearing.

Wish I could be there with you? She could be here. She could totally be here. Right now.

My thumbs pump out **Your decision** while my chest heaves. I click the send arrow so fast and with such enthusiasm, it's shocking how helpless I feel doing it.

I stick my phone deep in my coat pocket, hobble across the lobby through the side door into Starbucks, and get in line.

Shit. Shit. Shit.

My heart slides farther into my stomach as the barista happily asks what they can get me.

I order Dr. Sowah and me Mocha Frapps, and then wait for them while my phone lies still in my pocket. *Her decision.*

It was her decision. It's why she isn't answering my text. She knows it. But I know something, too. I know I wanted it to be her decision for the same reason she's always made everything mine. You'd think understanding your mother for the first time ever might actually feel good, but it doesn't. It sucks. I snatch out a Roxy and take it. Fuck being in pain.

The nice Starbucks server secures the Frapps into a to-go holder so I can carry them easily with one hand. Dr. Sowah loves Mocha Frapps. I'm not bringing him one *because* I need him to write me another prescription, I'm bringing him one *and* I need him to write me another prescription. Either way, I always bring him one because I like him, and he likes his Frapp.

As I'm heading toward the bank of elevators, my phone begins to vibrate.

I fumble between my forearm crutch and my pocket in my hurry to answer it, to speak to her, to tell her I'm sorry.

"Eve?"

Shit, it's Thomas Aquinas.

I hang up.

And then press for the elevator, hard, like twenty times, as if its arrival can somehow take me away from what just happened. Before it comes, my phone starts vibrating again. I don't even look. I know it's him. Of course it's him. Only Thomas Aquinas would call again. I can't stand it. Maybe it's her. I look. It's him.

My hand moves to my lips as I think about his lips.

Where is the damn elevator?

My phone keeps vibrating.

Oh, my fucking god, I hate Thomas Aquinas. Why didn't he text? I could be trying to rest right now. I could be asleep. I've just had goddamn surgery.

My phone stops. Finally. And I breathe a sigh of relief as the elevator opens in front of Dr. Sowah's reception desk.

Leslie, his receptionist, looks up and hoots, "Eve!"

"Hey, Leslie." I'd fall into her arms, if only I were able to.

Coming out from behind the desk, Leslie looks my body up and down, and reports, "You look great straight, girl! You're superlate, by the way." She then gives me an air hug, takes the holder with the Frapps, and leads me straight through the waiting room and down the hall, grabbing my chart off the desk as she walks past it.

We bump into Vardan, one of Dr. Sowah's nurses, halfway down the hall.

"Look at this one," he muses, giving me two air-kisses, one on each cheek. They're obviously used to spinal surgery patients—we live in fear of contact. "I'll take her," he says to Leslie. They exchange the Frapp holder and chart, and Vardan leads me into Radiology. "Put this on, honey," he says, throwing a gown onto the large steel-framed X-ray bed. "Will you need help?"

"I got it," I tell him.

"Give me your coat."

I gladly hand it over to him, relieved to be rid of my phone still in its pocket. He flips my coat over his arm and motions with the Frapps. "These will be waiting in the exam room," he says, and leaves.

I kick my sweats under the chair next to my shoes and hang my hoodie on the back of the door. I hate taking off my body sock. So I don't. They can X-ray through it.

With my brace still on, I put on the gown and lean against the X-ray bed, not fully committing to sitting down. The stillness and quiet remind me how exhausted I am, and I wish myself back in my bed, between my four green walls, surrounded by the familiar spray of collages.

He was calling about the kiss. That goddamn kiss. Anyway, I need to focus on why I'm here. The Roxy. What doctor would say no? He knows I need it.

Sighing, I commit to sitting by sliding back onto the table—it's more uncomfortable, not less. I want this to be over and I want more Roxy.

Someone knocks, and I answer, "Come in," like it's my home.

A tech swooshes into the room. She's got frizzy blond hair and large-framed black glasses. I never know the techs. She's nice but all business. She helps me out of my brace, and for the next twenty minutes, I follow her instructions to slide up, or down, or over. Clutch sandbags in front of my groin. Lift my arms over my head. Don't breathe. Breathe. Turn more to the right. Now, the left. And hold back an embarrassed laugh when she tries to mold a part of me to fit better in her machine. She is physically squishing me—a human, a person—like my body is a thing.

How many twisted young women has she seen today? Skinny. Tall. Ponytailed, braided, bobbed, buzzed, or 'froed females holding their breath while the machine's throaty buzz captures the glowing white of our bones. I've spent way too much time in front of an X-ray camera. Forget a crooked spine, I should be growing a third eye by now with all this exposure.

Vardan knocks. It's time. My heart rate picks up.

The tech disappears while Vardan helps me back into my sweatpants and brace—like Mary Fay, the man's an expert. We head down the hall to the exam room together.

I sip my Frapp, listening to Vardan chatter away while he takes my vitals. When it's time to step up onto the giant scale, his chitchat stops, and he frowns at the very low red number glaring at us from atop the machine. "Hm" is all he says. His frown deepens.

"Measure me," I say, changing the subject.

"Okay, okay, let's get to the fun part," he teases. When he takes the measurement, he yelps with joy. "You are five foot eight inches. That's over a two-inch post-surgery gain!"

I wince at his loud voice.

"In pain, sweetie?" he asks. I don't deny it. "Let's get that doctor in here to see you so you can jet." He sticks my chart in the chart box on the exam room's door and is gone. I wish he had closed the door. I need a moment to myself, to compose myself, to—

"Well, well, well," Dr. Sowah says, walking in. "If it isn't Eve Abbott. The smoker."

"Ha ha," I say, handing him his Frapp. My mouth twitching just a bit.

"So," he says, slurping his coffee, "let's talk about quitting, shall we?"

"Funny."

He gives me an affectionate tap on the top of my head with my chart and then opens it.

"Feeling okay?" he asks, reading the notes.

"Tired," I tell him.

"You should be getting some of your stamina back. But your weight is down. Are you eating?"

"Yes," I lie.

"And the pain?"

I shrug. Not trusting myself to do or say anything else.

There's a knock at the door. Dr. Sowah grunts, and it opens to Vardan carrying my films. Dr. Sowah takes them and shuts the door, and then sticks them up one at a time onto the light board with a thunk, thunk, thunk.

Then he switches on the light and...

Holy shit.

I instinctively scooch away from the screen, hugging my brace. Of course I knew about the bars running up alongside my spine, and the one, two, three, four, five, six, seven, eight—eight!—giant screws attaching the bars to my spine. And about the plate to which the whole thing was attached, screwed in down by my hips.

I knew.

But seeing? Seeing is something else.

"Look at me," I whisper. Not really believing what I'm seeing.

"I do good work, right?" He smiles.

"You sure do a lot of it," I say, responding to all the instrumentation crammed into me. "There's basically a bunch of scaffolding inside me."

Dr. Sowah chuckles. Then he points to different areas, highlighting the process of my fusion and where I am with it. I nod and make some sounds of agreement while I drink my Frapp, yet I can't take my eyes off the tilting mess now holding me upright. Weirdly, it looks haphazard. Not the neat job I was expecting.

"The good news is, you're fusing." He flips off the light. "Now let's see those incisions."

I unbrace and lie down. Dr. Sowah takes one last long suck from the Frapp before he puts it on the counter and peels back my body sock.

"Incisions look good for seven weeks post-op," he says. He gets up and rummages in a nearby cabinet. "I'll get these out."

"Now?" I ask.

"It'll be faster than you think, Eve. And it's time."

He gloves up and brings over a scissors-looking instrument and a giant sterile pad. "It's not painful," he adds.

I stare at him.

He chuckles. "At least, that's what I've been told."

I lie back and fix my eyes on the lights in the ceiling. He gets to work, beginning on the lower right side of my stomach. I can feel pinching, but that's about all. He's right. It doesn't hurt, although I don't tell him. I'm usually pretty talkative with Sowah. Not today.

"So, your mom get off okay? She e-mailed me that she was traveling."

She let him know she was going away?

"Yeah," I say, a tinge of love mixed with guilt fizzing in my stomach.

"You should be showering now."

"I took one yesterday. Can't you tell?"

He sniffs in big. "Like a rose."

I smile.

"When are you starting back to school? I can't quite remember the date we set. This week or next?"

My smile fades instantly. It was this week, but I don't feel the need to tell him about my bargain with Mary Fay. "Monday," I say, trying pretty unsuccessfully to keep my tone from sounding utterly depressed.

Dr. Sowah looks up from his scissors. "You don't need to stay all day, Eve. You can wade in, see what a few classes feel like. It's going to be the sitting that tires you. Don't overdo it or you'll end up back in pain."

A second mention of pain.

It's time.

I have to ask.

But I don't. I can't.

Dr. Sowah keeps working. There are a lot of staples. He starts to hum some song that I know although I can't place it. It's bugging me, but I let him alone.

School drifts back into my mind. This does not lift my spirits. Especially with Personal Development first period.

Personal Development was her idea. Goddamn it, Lidia. And now the kiss. Did I really have to go and make out with Thomas Aquinas?

What was I thinking?

I wasn't thinking, that's the point. I'll just explain that to him—that it was the drugs.

The drugs.

I have to ask for the drugs.

Again, I don't.

Instead, I envision myself trying to explain to Thomas Aquinas why I attacked him in the middle of the toilet paper aisle at the Stop & Shop. I remember the taste of him, and that moment when he kissed back—

"Eve?" Dr. Sowah's hands hover over my rib cage.

"What?"

"You just flinched. Did I pinch you?"

"No, no," I mumble.

The crunchy medical paper crinkles beneath me.

"You all right?" Dr. Sowah asks.

"Yeah."

But I'm not. Because I want that Roxy. I need it.

"Just another minute," he says, concentrating.

It's now or...now.

"Dr. Sowah?" I stretch my arms up over my head, trying to give off the look of someone who couldn't care less about the next thing they're about to say. "I'm kinda low on the Roxanol."

"You shouldn't be," he says.

I crack open my lips. Just a centimeter. I need the extra

air to slow my pulse. I close my eyes and try to conjure up calm things like birds flying and ocean waves.

"Well, maybe my mom left the other bottle in her bedroom. When I spoke to her yesterday, she couldn't remember where she put it, and I couldn't find it."

Great. An outright lie. When I'd googled *drug-seeking behaviors* last night, I'd promised myself I wouldn't do this.

"I'll renew. But we will need to talk about coming off the opioids, Eve, and your future pain management." His voice hits my skin as he speaks, tickling me. "There is a very real risk of dependency."

"Yeah," I say with a sleepy air. Like I don't care. Like talking about the Roxy is boring and not worth my time. And then I close my eyes and struggle not to cry. Because I did it. I have it. No matter that I had to lie. To push Mary Fay away. And my mother.

Every time I help you, Eve, a tiny piece of Minnesota will disappear.

For the first time ever, I see that it is. Disappearing. But it's not my mother who is in danger, it's me. It's been me all along.

I am Minnesota.

Dr. Sowah straightens up in his chair. "Done," he announces, checking his watch. "Record time, too."

"You were timing yourself?"

"It makes it fun." He smiles. "Now, let's get you on your way." And he grabs his prescription pad.

The Roxy.

I wait for the sting of joy. It doesn't come.

Possibly. Hopefully. Probably.

"Eve?"

It's Lidia.

"I'll be right out."
We're in the women's bathroom at
the movie theater and I'm holding
a giant fruit basket. It's a
real struggle to squish out
of the stall with it.

"Oh my god, Eve,
fruit!" she gushes, as if
fruit were the most wonderful
thing in the world.

She plucks out a pear
(her favorite, my least) and
bites into it. Leaning the basket against
the bathroom sink, I also pick out a pear and
take a bite.

This is a dream.
I would never eat a pear
in real life.

While I chew, I think about how I want to stay
    in here
forever, chomping on this yucky pear with Lidia.
But she turns to leave, to walk out.

"Don't!"

She stares back at me as the door closes, and
it's like I've never looked into those eyes in my
    entire life.
I don't know those eyes.
I've never seen those eyes.

The fluorescent lighting darkens and
I'm standing alone in the hallway
at school with the taste of
gross pear in my mouth.

Lidia is walking toward me. The
way she sways, her long stride, the
slope of her shoulders—
everything that sang out so
happy and familiar.
Once.

She grows closer.
I can't make out
her face. Yet I know, by the
way she sways, her long stride, the
slope of her shoulders—
that this is now a nightmare.

My eyes on the ground,
I let her pass. Without a word.
Leaving only the faint movement
of hair on my arm to know
she'd been there.

———

I wake myself with a whimper.

Alone in my dark room, I stare up at my ceiling. Wet. Cold. Bloated with fear.

Or is it grief?

Whatever it is, it writhes inside me, and god, it fucking hurts. I replace the coarse moistness of pear with the bitter chalkiness of Roxy. So much better. I start counting the minutes.

I once read that five minutes after the end of a dream, we have forgotten 50 percent of the dream's content. And ten minutes later, we've forgotten 90 percent. I wait…thinking how I wish this natural fizzling out of memory worked in real life, and that when we chose, we could forget our experiences five minutes after they happened.

Although I'm sure some asshole would say that these experiences are the ones that make us stronger or build our character.

Strength. Character. Key words for feeling like shit.

Maybe the people who can "bounce back" are actually just good at forgetting, as if they'd been dreaming and then woke up. Or the opposite: Instead of waking, they choose to sleep.

The minutes add up. I'm forgetting. I'm fine with it. Fine. I like the fading. It's soft.

And forgiving.

I need my phone.

The harsh light makes me blink. It's after two in the morning. I text anyway.

I'm sorry.

Dropping the phone onto my bed, I reach for my water. Even the memory of pear is too much.

A text buzzes back, shocking me.

A heart emoji.

It's amazing how perfect a red heart can be. She follows it with two more texts.

I moved my lecture.

I'll be home three days early.

I send her back my own heart emoji. And then I have an idea.

Can I stay out of school until then?

I watch the bubbles pulsating....

Spoke to MF. No.

My mother finally comes around and her first act of motherhood in forever bites me in the ass.

My thumbs hover dangerously over my phone, itching to text her that whether I am ready to attend school should be "my decision," but...that heart emoji. Instead, I send an angry cat face, toss down my phone, and close my eyes. She hates cats.

⸻

"Eve!"

It's Mary Fay. It can't possibly be morning.

It can't.

I don't move or answer. Because I am far away. Possibly I am gone. Possibly. Hopefully. Probably.

I hear her footsteps approach my bed. Her finger pokes me in the shoulder.

"Eve?"

I am not gone.

Anywhere but Here

I'D RATHER BE ANYWHERE BUT ON MY WAY TO SCHOOL IN Thomas Aquinas's car. He obviously senses this and asks, "Would you be more comfortable in the back seat?"

"Do you plan on driving erratically?"

He laughs. "I might," he says. "If you provoke me."

Facing the passenger-side window where he can't see, I roll my eyes.

I begged Mary Fay to let me stay home one more day. She wasn't having it. The woman absolutely knew it wasn't one day I wanted, but forever, even if she didn't know why. She also straight out told me that lying in my bedroom all weekend staring at a telescope had not helped my case.

Had I been staring?

So when Thomas Aquinas called Mary Fay this morning volunteering to pick me up, I knew I was doomed.

The sun is weakly shining. Cars and buses surround us. People wait to cross at lights, bags over arms. Others walk speedily past one another up and down sidewalks. A moving, active world. A world I'll be subjected to all day long in a body that I have no idea how to navigate. I have become the hamburger—forever wrapped inside its giant plastic head. But I'm still in here. Small, sweaty, and sans one salty french fry friend.

Thomas Aquinas takes a sharp right.

I lurch toward him. He quickly sticks out his hand to steady me, then pulls his hand back like I've burned him. And maybe I have because the place where he touched my arm stings with heat. He had called at least six more times since MGH. Because of course he would. Because he's Thomas Aquinas.

I picked up none of them.

He clears his throat, keeping his eyes on the road.

"You good?"

I let go of a big gulp of air.

"Yeah," I say, peeking over at him.

I should be kinder to Thomas Aquinas.

"Listen, Eve, I read over your crit essay for English Lit. You might want to take a look at your comma usage."

I glare out the windshield. I hate Thomas Aquinas.

"I like my commas right where they are."

"Missing?" he asks.

"What?"

"You didn't use any commas, Eve. And you needed them."

"According to who?"

"According to the rules of grammar."

He throws on his blinker as he pulls into the student parking lot and I shiver at the sight of so many cars and people and colors dodging about under the spindly trees that look even spindlier without their leaves. There's something so sad about parking lot trees.

"Anyway, I put them in for you."

"What?"

"The commas. I put them in, along with a few other minor adjustments."

"I don't need commas. I purposely did not put them in. That essay was exactly how I wanted it to be. It didn't need to be helped or fixed or changed."

Why am I getting so upset at him over an essay I can barely remember writing?

"Chill, Eve. It's just an essay."

And now, I'm pissed again. Only *I* can say it's just an essay.

He gets out of the car and shuts his door. I open my door and there he is, reaching down to help.

"I can do it," I grumble.

"As you wish, Eve. I shall stand here with the easy ability to aid you in your exit from the vehicle yet will not endeavor to do so."

I ignore him, struggling to get out of his car, but my body is a log wrapped in hard plastic and his car is too low. I'm stuck.

"Why is your car dragging on the ground?"

He says something about his car and standards although I'm not hearing him because now I'm struggling to reach behind me for my backpack in the back seat. Which—because I am completely fused is completely impossible.

"What the fuck, Eve!" He leans past me and grabs my backpack.

"You have the worst mouth," I say.

"You didn't seem to mind my mouth Tuesday night in the Stop & Shop." He grins.

Oh. No. He. Did. Not.

"Yeah, well, I was on drugs."

"Creo que sigues endrogada."

"Don't think I didn't get that."

"I absolutely know you did not get that"—he laughs—"since you're failing Spanish."

I hate him. And not just because he's right. Okay, totally because he's right.

I make a second attempt to get out of his outrageously low car. "Don't touch me."

He steps back. "You do you, Eve," he says.

I scoot all the way to the end of the seat and then feel around for something to give me leverage. I'm cursing myself for not bringing my forearm crutches, especially since the only reason I left them home was to spite Mary Fay—if she was going to make me return, I was going to make it as hard as possible on myself to spite her. I'm pretty damn sure she didn't even notice.

Velcroed tightly inside my post-surgery brace and without anything to push off of, I basically topple out of the car toward the pavement. Thomas drops my backpack and catches me.

I hate his hands on me. I hate him pulling me up without

any effort. I hate the way he makes a show of brushing me off after he sets me on my feet.

"Cut it out."

"You need a sense of humor," he says with a cheerful snort.

"I need my backpack. And BTW, I'm taking paratransit home. Your car is a death trap."

He shakes his head, taking the math textbook out of my backpack. "I'll return this to DeSota for you." Then he zips the bag back up and hands it to me.

All it has in it now is my spiral notebook and my English Lit paper. His English Lit paper. I start toward the front doors.

He walks next to me.

"You can stop in the library and reprint your essay without my corrections during Personal Development first period," Thomas says. "I don't even know what that class is, so it can't be important."

"Personal Development is a perfectly fine class," I snap. Although I remember how Lidia had dubbed it *Personal Downtime*. She'd chosen it as a place for us to hang together. "Anyway, why the hell do you know my schedule by heart? That's mega-creepy."

I can see his smirk out of the corner of my eye. "We basically have the same schedule, my dear School Within a School pal. Except of course for Personal Development. Which you obviously need."

I don't respond. His comment is below me. Plus, I don't have a comeback that won't just make him sound more right.

The crowd ahead of us slows due to the traffic jam at the

front doors. I teeter a bit as the space around me shrinks. Every-one is too close to the throbbing sore newness of my spine. To my sawed-off ribs. To the thin, soft skin of my incisions.

Way too close.

I stumble. Thomas reaches for me, but I catch myself and back away. Elbows, hoodies, bags... even their cheerful shouts are threatening.

"Listen, I'm going to wait out here until everyone goes in," I tell him.

He stands there for a second, staring at me. And I know he's thinking he should wait with me but is most likely afraid to suggest it because I'll bite his head off. I most likely would. *Friends*, he'd mouthed, standing in my living room. I don't deserve a friend.

"I'll be fine. You go on in."

He stands there for another second, like he might not listen to me, then nods and moves on. I watch the back of his jean jacket disappear into the crowd of bodies and suddenly feel more alone than I have since that night at the movies. Two months... it feels like two hundred years.

I wander back toward one of the benches under the front office windows, and, slapping my empty-ish backpack on the bench, I lower myself down next to it.

A couple of people say happy hellos and welcome backs as they pass. I mumble hi in return but pull myself deeper into my brace to keep them walking.

The first bell rings, sounding more like a very loud board game buzzer than a bell. The crowd gets louder and picks up speed as it makes for the doors. They only have four minutes before they need to be in homeroom—I doubt anyone expects me on time, or at all.

The second bell rings and I'm still on the bench. The murmur inside the school quiets. A cold spring breeze whips by, clanking together the branches of the trees surrounding the student parking lot and making everything feel hollow.

I put half a Roxy in my mouth and let it dissolve, savoring the chalkiness as I watch the birds fly out of the trees together in one big clump, only to spin about in the air and re-land like some strange version of a bird flash mob. The Roxy tastes extra-terrible, which feels somehow right to me. I only take halves now. Although sometimes I still take two halves. This morning was sometimes.

I look around but am actually seeing her...willing her to come to me. To be here. To take me inside. To help me through this day.

My face feels like it's sliding off me. I don't have long until my whole body will slide off this bench. The world begins to blur. Or maybe I begin to blur.

Don't blur, Eve.

I open my eyes. Wide. Taking in the trees, the sky. The birds? Where are the birds? My eyes are closed.

School. You're at school, Eve. God, I just want to be fucking anywhere but here.

No.

Not anywhere.

Not there.

The Real One

You didn't move.
Unlike Jayden,
who flew up out of his chair.
The hat—
the one he'd so sweetly
placed on your head
twelve minutes earlier—
spiraling out into the darkness.

"What the hell!"
he whispered.
"What the hell.
What the hell.
What the hell."
Hoarsely,
in fear.
Fear.

Stumbling about
between the seats,
the action on the movie screen
flickered across his T-shirt

while shouts of disapproval
peppered the air.

I tried to stand, too.
But Nick's gruff voice
held me in place.
"Sit the fuck down,"
he said to Jayden.
Obviously pissed.
Obviously already putting up
with quite enough
just being here.
Obviously having no idea
what the hell was going on.

Jayden dumped himself
into his chair, and
once again,
we were separated.

On screen, tropical trees
bent sideways in
hurricane-force winds while
rain pounded a broiling sea and the
blades of a helicopter
beat against the sound system.
The world was being

blown apart and there was
nothing I could do but
watch it happen.

Your heads moved together.
Ear to ear. Cheek to cheek. It was
your voice I heard.
Whispering hoarsely.
In fear.
Fear.

I couldn't hear the words,
not that they mattered.
What mattered was him.
Jayden of the grin.

He looked down in your lap.
The whispers continued.
The movie continued.
Nick continued to watch the screen,
oblivious of the tension around him.
In fact, he looked relaxed. The movie
making him forget
about me.

Suddenly,
Jayden of the grin stood up and
my heart dropped

to the sticky theater floor. But
he didn't push past me. Instead,
he leaned deeply over the seats
and retrieved the hat.
For you.

In this small exchange,
I saw your face for the first time.

Triumphant.

You'd taken the chance,
and it had worked out.
Proving once again,
Lidia Banks never needed two hands. Lidia Banks
never needed two hands. Lidia
Banks never needed
two hands. LidiaBanksne
verneededtwoh
andsLid
iaBan
ksne
vernee
dedtwo
hands.

I'll Be Waiting

Lurching awake, I quickly wipe the drool from my mouth and look around to be sure no one saw me sleeping before I stumble inside the school dragging both my backpack and my head.

"Hey, missy." Ms. Kisner, the school nurse, calls everyone "missy." "Spine not okay?"

She swooshes back a curtain revealing a cot where I lie down, shoes and all. She talks for a bit, covers me with a blanket. Her voice is kind, high-pitched. Her sneakers squeak now and then as she makes her way around her office. Drawers slide in and out. A crowd hums in the distance... then all is silent. I think I hear the birds again. Chirping. I definitely hear the birds.

And then I feel him.

"Eve," he says.

I'm smiling now.

I'm happy now.

He's what I need right now.

I keep my eyes closed, afraid he won't be there if I open them. I hear him sit in the chair near my cot and imagine him crossing his arms in front of him. He has nice arms. Big arms. I feel them catching me outside of school this morning.

Wait. What? Not his arms.

Those were not his arms.

"What's wrong, Eve?"

His voice? I don't know whose voice.

"Nothing." I sigh, my eyes still closed. "I'm just busy trying to figure out exactly how out of my mind I am."

"I'll help you," he says. "Way out."

The warmth in his voice makes me feel
close to him. Connected.
The buzzer ends a class period.
"I better go," he says.
"Don't."

Silence surrounds the word,
surrounds us—a silence
neither of us fill.

———

He leans nearer. I can feel his presence pressing in on me.

"I'll be waiting, after school. Under the portico." He

whispers it—and I remain perfectly still, experiencing every beautiful syllable.

I hear him stand, move away. And feeling a little braver, although not brave enough to open my eyes, I say, "Don't show up all cool on a motorcycle or something."

He laughs. The sound of it tingles down the scaffolding attached to my spine, and for a second...less than a second even, I'm hoping.

An Exact Replica

Ms. Kisner is gently shaking my arm, suggesting I try attending a class or two.

School.

I'm at school.

Yawning, I roll off the cot and use one of the nurse's paper water cones to take a Roxy, sipping slowly, putting off the inevitable—going out there.

By the time I arrive at English Lit, the class is in full swing. Miss Mason stops lecturing.

"Hey, Eve, welcome back."

I nod and take my seat, avoiding eye contact with Thomas Aquinas while attempting to shrug off the attention Mason is throwing my way.

She immediately understands. "Okay, let's get back to transcendentalism."

Oh, how I need Thomas Aquinas's paper! Especially

because I most likely am not going to listen to a word of this lecture.

I open my notebook and fuss about trying to find a way to tolerate the hard chair. Then I fix my gaze up at the front of the room . . . and think about him.

I'll be waiting.

Like a date.

No. Not a date. This isn't a date.

It's just him . . . in the human form. So I sit in class, walk through the halls, sit in the next class, answer a question or two, pop another Roxy or two—I *don't want to overdo it and end up back in pain*, as per my doctor—even throw an opinion out about something. Because he will be there. Waiting. And I smile.

In fact, I spend the rest of the day smiling.

They say your own attitude can change everything. Well, I might have to start believing these *they* people because *they* are right. It seems that an Eve flashing her carefree self all through the halls is an Eve everybody needs to chat up. I'm late to every class because I'm extremely busy being greeted by everyone and being told how good I look.

Inside the classroom, I double down on the joy by picturing *him* waiting outside for me, while the other one sits behind me.

When Mr. Bogdani calls on me in Gov, I confess I don't know what the heck is going on.

"Good drugs, right, Eve?" Rodney Papageorgiou calls out.

"Yes," I admit.
The whole class cracks up. Even Mr. B.
I feel a slight kick at the back of my chair and ignore it.
"May I use the bathroom, Mr. B.?
"At your leisure," he answers.

The hall is eerily quiet.
I meant to head to the water
fountain but take a
wrong turn or two,

or
three.

I'm in no hurry, just
contentedly wandering
when I round a corner and
find myself in front of
Lidia's locker.

She is there.
Surrounded by a small
crowd, along with
her hand.

Her hand.

I step back against the lockers in surprise.

She is explaining how
the hand is an
exact replica of her
real hand.
How she sent a
million pictures
of her existing hand
to the company.

I took those pictures.

"I can even paint
the fingernails."

We bought a
shit ton of nail polish
that afternoon.

I wrap my arms around
my brace, the only
thing holding me
together.
Without it
my heart, my lungs, my intestines
would splash out
onto the stained brown carpet.

When I blink, Lidia
and I are standing
in the hall
alone.

"Lid!" I croak.
She looks up and
smiles that Lidia smile that shows up in
her eyes even more than
her mouth.

"Eve," she says. "You
look great!"

My heart soars.
Soars.

"Lidia, Lidia, Lidia,"
I sing.

"Eve," she
groans. But it's her
loving groan. I
love her
loving groan.

I struggle
to hold back

a hundred more happy
*Lidia*s
while she swings
her backpack over her shoulder, and
using her new hand,
slams the metal locker
shut.

———

The bell is ringing. I look around at Ms. Kisner's office, hearing the scratchy sound of the cot paper beneath my head.
The halls fill with whoops and shouts—end-of-the-day
kinds of whoops and shouts. I lie on the cot, knowing I've
been here all along.

The Real One

You stood before the credits
started to roll. Jayden stood,
too, stretching slowly, like he was
some sort of grandfather
leaving his overstuffed chair
after hours of watching TV.

I waited for Nick to stand,
but he didn't.
He kept his eyes on the screen
like he was super-interested in the credits,
though I knew he was
just putting off reentry into a world where he
might have to interact
with me. So I stood—
using Jayden's technique—
pretending to stretch.

I peeked over but
purposely avoided your eye.
Knowing you wouldn't want me
looking at you, making sure you were okay.
Because you

were okay.
You were
always okay.

Finally,
Nick rose to his feet with a long sigh,
as if I needed
another signal
that this night wasn't going
well for him.

Although, even in this act of standing,
Nick took his time,
and Jayden,
at an obvious loss for what to do
with these extra moments,
turned around in the aisle and
adjusted the black fedora
at a jaunty angle
on your head.

You smiled up at him
from under the brim, and
my heart nearly exploded.
That smile. The one that showed up more in your eyes
than your mouth, a smile that said,
The whole fucking world is mine.
It's all mine.

How could he not be in awe of you?
I'd always been in awe of you.

I followed Nick up the aisle and
through the theater hallway
toward the front concession stand
without looking back. I
wanted to look back. I was
dying to look back.

I also felt
completely weird
shuffling after this absolute asshole
who refused to acknowledge my existence.
So when you called out for me to wait,
I was thrilled.

You needed to use the bathroom.
I did, too,
though I didn't feel like
I had enough power to ask.
This was the difference between us,
Lidia.
Power.
You were so
powerful.
You called me back
and I came.

You called Jayden and Nick back
and they came.

We left them standing
across from the bathrooms
by a giant cardboard cutout of
two cartoon aliens. Nick
crumpled to the carpeted floor
next to the advertisement. Jayden
leaned against the windowsill, arms folded.
You and I
headed in.

Just before the door closed,
you playfully took the hat from your head and
tossed it over to Jayden.
"Think fast." You laughed.
He caught it and
grinned.

Take Me Somewhere

It's quiet in the nurse's bathroom and safe from the after-school hordes streaming through the hallways. Safe. Sitting on the closed toilet seat. All I need to do is stay in this bathroom. Five more minutes? Six? Who knows how long it takes to change everything.

But bathrooms are temporary. You can't stay in them forever.

"You all right in there?" Nurse Kisner calls, proving my point.

"Yes." My voice bounces off the close walls, shocking me. Temporary.

But I'm not ready to leave.

Still playing at normalcy, I begin to fool around with my hair in the mirror. Pulling out my hair tie, I fluff it up a bit. Yet it hangs all wonky, so I twist it back on top of my head in the same messy bun I had it up in when I entered. My eyes pass quickly over my face and land on my brace.

It's difficult to see how different I look with it on. Difficult, though not impossible.

Nineteen degrees.

The Velcro echoes off the tile. My shirt, a wrinkled mess. I pull it over my head. Toss it on top of the brace sitting upright on the floor, leaving me in a body sock and sweats. A body sock hugging my body. My body that is different. I look different. Everything is different. Just like she knew it would be.

I'm back in my brace with my shirt on and another half a Roxy in my mouth before I even remember doing it. I suck on this one. Wanting to punish myself for the incredible feeling already pulsing through me that everything is right in the world, yet...I'm sitting locked in a bathroom. And the funny thing is, even this thought can't break through the everything's-right-in-the-world feeling.

Picturing him out there waiting. That breaks through. A bit. And I suck harder on my Roxy.

"Miss Abbott? Either you come out or I come in."

He is leaning on a light-gray minivan under the portico, between a line of yellow buses. Reading a book. His long hair is tied back, and his gold-framed glasses sit at the end of his nose. He's completely absorbed, although the din under the massive portico is wild with shouts, laughter, and the deafening roar of the last school buses pulling out.

He? Him? Thomas Aquinas? Do I care who?

No. I don't. I do. I do care.

I'm just about to turn around, find another bathroom to never come out of when he looks up. His eyes find mine, and I don't turn around.

I walk slowly toward him,
confident,
because I am looking out
through the grinning
teeth of a hamburger.

He stares back at me,
with a straight-on smile.
Acknowledgment.
Approval.
Acceptance.

"Better than a motorcycle?" he asks, waving his hand at the minivan behind him.

"Not much."

My body is stiff—not from metal rods and plates but from fear.

"You really are a complete coconut, Eve." He laughs as he takes my backpack from me and opens my door.

I need to place my hand on his forearm to hoist myself up into the van. The warmth of him creeps right up my arm, through my chest, and up into my neck and cheeks. I let go, scooting onto the seat.

He hands me my backpack. "See," he says, raising his eyebrows, "easy-peasy getting in, huh?"

"How could I have ever thought you were the devil?" I ask him, before I can stop myself.

"Aw," he says, "an Eve compliment. Thank you." And he closes my door.

The quiet sends a shiver down my spine. A shiver that doesn't hurt. His close presence is wedging itself in between the nerves in my body. No message. No pain. He opens his door, gets in, and shuts it, and I'm enclosed. With Thomas Aquinas.

He starts the van. I can't take my eyes off his hand on the stick shift, a terrible urge washes over me to reach out, to place my palm over his thick knuckles. The thought has me pulling my eyes away from his side of the van altogether and staring out my own window, fogging it up with my breath.

It starts to rain. The movement of the van and the long day catch up to me. And maybe that last Roxy. I lean back and close my eyes. As soon as I do, I see her smiling in front of her locker. She's wearing the fedora.

"Take me somewhere."

My voice bounces off the window.

He clears his throat. "What?"

I can't turn my head toward him. I can't face him. "Take me somewhere," I repeat, placing my hands in my lap. "Somewhere you go when you want to be alone."

He doesn't say anything...though I feel the acceleration of the van, and another mile later, we do not take the turn onto Ashmont toward home. I'm going wherever he takes me.

He drives smoothly, making every turn and downshift with my spine in mind. Did he hear the loneliness in my voice? Is he done with me now? Like her?

We pull out onto the interstate.

———————

We drive without speaking for what feels like a very long time. The wind blows the rain against the windows. I might have fallen asleep. Or maybe this is all a dream. I don't even care if it is. I look over at him. He keeps his eyes on the road.

"The glass museum," I think he says, but I'm not sure.

"What?" I ask.

"We're going to the glass museum, in New Bedford."

"A glass museum."

He takes a quick look at me from the side of his gold rims.

"We don't have too long. It closes at five."

I look at the van's clock. It's 3:30 p.m. "We have an hour and a half," I say. "In glass-museum time, that's like six days!"

He laughs. "Glass is cool. It's useful *and* beautiful. What else can you say that about?"

"Underwear," I suggest.

" 'Underwear'?" he repeats, totally thinking about me in my underwear.

I look out my window. "Stop it," I say.

"What?" he says, grinning.

"You know."

"Thinking about you in useful and beautiful underwear?"

"Don't forget to picture all the scars," I say, wishing I hadn't.

"Can you describe them?" he asks. "Where they start from. Where they go to?"

"Just drive," I say, feeling every inch of my scars.

Five minutes later we pull into the glass museum's parking lot. There are only two cars in the lot.

"I hope we can get in," I say.

"You're going to like this place," he says.

I leave my backpack in the car. He opens the door for me. I let him help me out. He hurries me through the rain into the museum.

We stand in front of a ticket booth while he stomps the rain off him and I try to catch my breath. I haven't moved that quickly in months. The man in the booth looks up through his own gold-rimmed glasses.

Behind me, he pulls a card out of his wallet and shows the man behind the counter.

"Have a great time," the man says, waving us on.

We walk through a turnstile and into the museum. "You have a membership?" I whisper.

"Don't judge," he says.

We stop at the first big piece. It's a gold glass window-looking picture of a man wearing a crown and riding a fish.

"Edris Eckhardt," he says in my ear. His breath tickles and makes my entire head tingle. "It's called *The Four Horsemen*."

It's strange, yet pretty. I stand very still, hoping he'll whisper more.

Outside the museum windows, the rain continues to fall. Inside, the museum is warm and filled with glass cases—glass behind glass.

The rooms are small and lead into one another. Everything glows in yellow lights. The carpets stifle all sound. It's like a colorful cocoon.

He pulls me into a room that contains a series of stained-glass windows of what look like saints all done in collage. Men and women. Broken up and put back together. Maybe there is some deeper religious purpose, although all I see are the brilliant oranges, electric blues... and shapes, thousands of tiny shapes. All different. All perfectly placed—each one contributing to the whole. These are my brothers. My sisters. Pieced together in bright, jagged beauty. Standing in front of them, I feel as beautiful as they are. And I only move on when my spine begs me to.

Together and apart, Thomas Aquinas and I drift from room to room, from work to work, looking, reading. Sometimes he finds me next to something and whispers interesting facts about it and sometimes we just collectively stare. It's not all vases and goblets, which is what I thought it would be, but sculptures and windows and lamps and jewelry and syrup bottles.

The syrup bottles are fun. There is a whole wall of them, a big rainbow of funky shapes. I stand in front of them for a bit.

"I like these, too, Eve," he says.

It makes me shudder...the way he says my name.

We stare at the colorful display together, and the question just falls out.

"Why do you like me?"

His eyes scan the bottles, like he's looking for the one with the right answer. His hesitation has me folding up inside.

But then there's something about the way he holds his shoulders, the stillness of his chest, his lips stretching out just the smallest bit.

"You're interesting."

He says it to the display, not me.

"I'm 'interesting'?" I repeat, grinning. And I admit, in a pretty goofy way.

He looks at me. "Don't get all syrupy."

I grin bigger. I might have tears in my eyes.

"Syrupy, because we're standing in front of syrup bottles."

"Come on," he says, grabbing my hand. "I better get you to the gift shop."

"I love gift shops," I say. And I do. I love everything right now. Because I'm interesting.

———

The gift shop is full of glass—of course—although in here we can touch it. It's weird how much fun it is to touch stuff. Although I don't pick anything up. Since the surgery, I've been noticing that the message from my brain to open and close my fingers doesn't seem to correspond well with the actual opening and closing of my fingers. Instead, I run my finger-tips down the sides of the vases, feel the vast smoothness of the giant bowls and platters, and clutch the chunky pendants in my fist right where they hang. When I find a pool of glass marbles, I plunge both my hands in and let the marbles filter through my fingers like loud, clanking, colorful flour. An electric-blue one catches my eye—the color that winked brightest at me from the glass collage of the saints. I pick it out from the pool and let it roll into the center of my palm.

"Look at this one, Thomas."

It's the first time I've called him by name. He seems to realize it, too, because he focuses all his attention on the marble. And as if not being able to stop himself from touching the beautiful piece of glass in my hand, he reaches out a finger and moves it gently in a circle around my palm, looking into the very center of it. The movement stops my breath and sends shivers crackling through me. I pull away.

"I'm going to get this one."

My legs shake as I head to the counter where the same man in glasses who checked us in waits to make the marble sale.

Thomas follows.

"Let me." He pulls out his wallet. "I get a fifteen percent discount with my membership."

I laugh, and it ends in a wide yawn. He notices.

"I'll get you home."

After he pays eighty-five cents for my marble, we turn to leave. We head out in the rain. It's almost dark, but the streetlights aren't on yet. The sky glows an eerie white.

I lumber as fast as possible toward the van and then literally crawl inside. He shuts the door. I sink back into the seat with my backpack in my arms and close my eyes.

Thomas climbs in the van, starts the engine. He's talking. His words sound sweet.

I want to respond, to say thank you, for the marble, for the museum...but it's too much work to bring up words from inside me and push them out. I hug my backpack and drift off as the the motion rocks me to sleep.

⸻

Mary Fay's voice reaches out through a fog.

"Homemade fish sticks in five."

Blinking, I look around. I'm on the couch. Mary Fay is banging about in the kitchen.

She pops her head into the living room. "Orange juice?"

I'm so confused.

"Oh, no. Cranberry, right?" she corrects.

"Yes, please, cranberry. I love cranberry," I blurt, attempting to hide the fact that I have no idea what is going on, what day it is, what time it is, and whether or not this is really happening. She disappears, and I drop my head back onto the couch.

How did I get here? Where had I been...somewhere.

With him.

Him?

My hand moves to my pocket, where I find it. The cool, hard glass of a marble, and the world lights up in electric blue. Because Thomas Aquino thinks I'm interesting.

Trying

"Morning, Metallica," Mary Fay says through a half-opened door. "Time to haul out the old saddlebags."

This woman does not stop. I ignore her and sink back into a gloriously deep sleep.

The light switches on.

I cry out in pain and hear her laugh from down the hall. "It's just morning, Eve. Not a colonoscopy."

Music blasts on from the kitchen.

I'm learning the easiest path with Mary Fay is to just do whatever she wants. Which sucks.

I throw back the covers and bring myself into a sitting position using a Nancy-taught technique—allowing gravity to work on the weight of my legs while I propel myself upright in a single motion.

My second motion is to reach for my orange bottle, but a bright blue marble catches my eye. And as my hand closes around the smooth glass, visions of beautiful saints, softly whispered words, and rows and rows of syrup bottles flood my head, and before I know it, I'm carrying a pretty polka-dot sweater and my favorite pair of skinny jeans out to the kitchen.

Mary Fay takes one look at them and sings, "We're trying, we're trying." And I tell her to quit it and just help me get them on, although I'm smiling. Because I am trying.

<hr />

This time, it's me, waiting for him. Standing at the bottom of my front steps. I'm sweating a little. It could be my buttoned-up coat on a warm spring morning, or it could be how hot my hands are in my pockets, one hand clutching a blue marble, or it could be that Thomas Aquino thinks I'm interesting. I'm interesting. My stomach flips with...hope.

Shit. It's true. I'm hoping. I'm hoping Thomas Aquino really does think I'm interesting. Because I like him. I like Thomas Aquino.

These thoughts jump around in my head, affecting my heart, my lungs, my entire body. I'm standing in a weird position—a position I want him to find me in when he pulls up. And as silly as it is, I'm too scared to reposition myself, like somehow he will see me do this. Though he isn't here.

He isn't here.

Cars roll by. None of them a gray minivan. Coldness spreads through me and the first remotely cute outfit I've worn in forever. I picture him waking up and remembering the museum, the syrup bottles, what he said. And then

I picture his face, crumbling. A mistake. He'd made a mistake. I was a mistake.

A gray minivan slows and pulls to the curb. I breathe. Breathe deeply. Tears stinging my eyes, at how incredible it feels. How incredible I feel.

He steps out of the van.

"Eve."

"Thomas."

We both laugh. He has a beautiful smile. I'd never noticed it before, his smile. I was always so afraid of it.

I climb into the van, feeling the warmth of that smile through the back of my rib cage.

We don't speak. I focus on the road to keep myself grounded while my thoughts flit about the museum, landing on color, shapes, him.

"Why do you always wear that T-shirt?"

He keeps his eyes on the road. There is clearly a reason.

"Were you born there? In Minnesota?"

He glances over at me. He's deciding. I look out my window so that my gaze doesn't stop him from saying what it is he's thinking of maybe not saying.

"My grandmother," he says.

"Was from Minnesota?"

"If by Minnesota you mean Puerto Rico." He laughs. "She brought my mom and my aunts to Boston when they were little. She was a . . . a great person. Anyway, whenever something went wrong, she'd always say 'Mañana, nos vamos a mudar a Minnesota.'"

I look back at his profile, waiting for the translation.

"Tomorrow, we're moving to Minnesota."

I cough out a laugh. Thomas smiles.

"Yeah, because nothing bad ever happens in Minnesota," I whisper, thinking about my mother. Thinking about how relieved I am that she'll be home soon.

"Anyway," he finishes, "she passed away at the beginning of ninth grade and I ordered a bunch of these T-shirts the next day." He turns to face me full-on, the confident Thomas grin back on his face. "I don't know a damn thing about hockey. I was just playing with you that day in your living room. I ordered it because it said 'Minnesota' and I like the color yellow."

He pulls under the busy portico.

"I'm sorry about your grandmother."

His hand lifts from the wheel as if he might reach over, touch me, but instead he runs his fingers through his hair and nods.

Maneuvering around all the buses, he pulls up right where he'd been waiting for me yesterday. Thomas Aquino. Leaning on the van. In his yellow shirt. Reading. What was the book? Poetry. He was reading poetry and waiting for *me*.

With my head full of him, I stagger out of the van, grabbing at the door handle. He's by my side. But he doesn't move, he waits. For me. To reach out for him.

His cheek is rough. His breathing shallow.

"Eve," he whispers.

My name. How can my name be the best sound I've ever heard in my entire life?

This time, *he* kisses *me*. Under the portico. With a hundred bus engines revving and a thousand voices ringing out around us. Just his lips. Softly tasting mine. The warm smell of him filling my nose.

When he stops—our mouths lingering close—I catch sight of myself in his eyes. I am so bright.

The echoing of a bus horn breaks us apart. Looking around at the crowd like they all just appeared out of nowhere and my lips still lit up with the feeling of his, I see her. Seeing me. Seeing that kiss.

Lidia.

Me and Lidia

The gym was still warm from
the work of many bodies.
And although the fluorescent lights
shone brightly overhead,
the darkness waiting for us
outside seemed to drift in and
dim the place.

Lidia was always last
from the locker room, but
I never minded.

The practice mat—lying in the
corner by the closed bleachers—was
my little island. It was a place
I got shit
done.

I'd written up my bio lab,
read my English chapters, and
finished the
pointless
worksheet for history.

All to the background hum of
sneakers squeaking and breathless
shouts punctuated by the
slap of volleyball against maple.

"You ready, weirdo?"
Lidia asked,
still flushed from practice,
clean hair dripping.

"Yup."

Lidia dribbled her volleyball
while I shoved away my books and
stood. Each bounce
following in perfect precision
to the last—even when she
wasn't watching but instead
noticing a face at the long
rectangular window in the gym door.

Thomas Aquino didn't see her because
Thomas Aquino was looking at me.

Lidia popped the ball
into the air and over to me
in a single motion,
missing my face only

because I knocked it back
in self-defense.
"Lid!"

"You gotta pay attention," she
said, sliding her backpack down
her arm to the floor.
"Try it this way."

Opening her palm, she
dropped the ball onto it from the
crook of her other arm,
popping it up
lightly
into the air.

Catching it,
she demonstrated a
few more times.
Pop, catch.
Pop, catch.
Pop, catch.
While my eyes
didn't dare
stray to the window.

"Ready?"

"Lid…"

"Ready?"

I sighed, dropping my backpack
to the floor with a clunk.
"Ready."

"Nice and easy,"
she said, serving.

I opened my palm
and smacked at
the ball.
It rocketed
directly at her face. She
ducked in the nick
of time.

"Whoops."
I laughed.

"Come on, Eve.
Try."

"I did
try."

"Try harder."

She popped
me the ball.

I did try harder.
I couldn't help it.

This time,
I hit it up and over
Lidia's head,
where it ricocheted
off two walls. Yet she
somehow
managed to return it.

I darted and,
despite my brace,
arrived in time to
slap at it sloppily.

The ball wobbled
but made its way
to Lidia.

There.
Done.

But Lidia wasn't
done.
Back it came.
Spiraling left.

I stumbled,
brace digging into rib,
rerouting it right before
it sailed past me.

She returned it,
again.
But this time
low and short. And
what seemed like suspiciously
on purpose.

I rushed forward,
scooping it up from where I'd
slid to my knees.
Almost missing it.
But not!

Up it flew
in a beautiful arc
where I felt every shade of
red,

orange,
yellow,
green,
blue,
indigo,
violet.
Until…

She broke off the game
with a catch.
"You're tired,"
she said.

Was I?

I glanced toward
the window, where I
saw a flash of gold glasses
disappear.
No.
No, I wasn't.

Dry

She takes off. I immediately go after her. Pretending I don't hear him. Calling me. Over and over. Instead, I concentrate on putting one foot in front of the other while avoiding the threat of random bodies as I struggle after her.

Once I'm through the doors, she's gone.

Lidia. Always the athlete.

I move around the corner and lean on the wall to catch my breath while I search the crowded hall outside the front office. But then I remember Thomas and head to the nurse's office.

"Hey, missy," says Ms. Kisner. "Day two not starting out well?" She's sitting at her desk stapling papers.

"The ride in was rough," I tell her, like I'd ridden to school on a boat or something.

The homeroom warning bell rings.

"I've got some admin errands to run. Take a load off for

a bit." She picks up her papers and heads out the door. "I'll check in on you in thirty."

I fill a paper cone with water and go into the bathroom. Again, the goddamn bathroom. I shut the door, put down the toilet seat, sit, and then reach for my Roxy.

Oh...my backpack. Where's my backpack?

Shit. Shit Shit.

My head swivels...searching the floor, my arms, my brace. Standing up, I turn and, holding on to the sink, look all around me, my heart pounding. It's not here. It's not in here.

Swinging open the bathroom door, I check the cot, the floor, the chair. Empty. Empty. Empty. They're all empty.

My panic growing, I reach out and violently swish back the curtain between the cot and Ms. Kisner's desk, knowing full well that my backpack is not out there, but I'm filled with the swirling energy of despair and have to do something.

I know where my backpack is. I know exactly where it is. I fucking left it in the van.

Jamming my hands into my coat pockets, just in case I somehow stuck one in there...wishing I had. Just one. Why didn't I think to stick one in here? I'd do anything to feel a plastic baggie. Anything. But the emptiness is so complete my fingers ram one another inside the pockets by the zipper.

Again, I search the chair, the cot, yanking the crinkling paper from it because it has given me nothing. Nothing. There is no Roxy here.

None.

I move toward the door. Should I go out to the van? Where is the van? What class has Thomas got first?

I feel his lips on mine but can't relive it without seeing her. Seeing the anger. The hate.

The late homeroom bell rings.

My head feels light. I lean heavily on the cot for a second, exhausted, but then my energy returns, and again, it hurts to stay still.

I walk out into the quiet hall and then back in again. The pacing isn't helping, so I roll onto the cot and lie blinking up at the white-and-gray drop ceiling. My lips feel dry. I lick them. Two seconds later I need to lick them again. Oh my god, I don't even have my ChapStick—but even thinking about ChapStick I'm picturing Roxy. I take a couple of breaths. Try to calm down.

Why did I have to leave that bag in his van?

The first-period bell rings, pouring everyone back into the hallway.

Shit. Thomas.

I roll off the cot and stand up.

I cup my hands together like I'm holding my Roxy. It doesn't help. I need my bottle. And what's wrong with that? My spine hurts, and I've had a major surgery.

I wrap my arms around my brace. I'm cold. I just want my bottle. Why did I leave it in the van? I took a half this morning, didn't I? I'm sure I did. It's in there. I'm sure it's in there. But my fear—it's eating it right out of my bloodstream, sucking the beautiful drug from my body. I close my eyes and tilt my face to the ceiling like it's the sun and try to breathe, try to slow down my heart from cranking out the Roxy into my blood where it can be slowly drained away. It's no use. I can't remember how to breathe. I can't slow my heart. And my nose is running.

The first-period late bell rings.

Thomas!

I just want my Roxy. I don't care about anything else. I just want it. I have to find the van.

I turn to leave and walk right into Lidia.

The Real One

You were glowing.
Your eyes,
your lips, even your
hair shone so brightly that
it nearly crackled with electricity.

When it was your turn
to use the bathroom,
you waved me ahead—
a drop of familiarity,
and I lapped it up.
Everything was going so well.
So well.

Why, then, did I feel
such a rush of relief
when I closed the stall door?

Peeing in a public restroom has
always been a process for me,
which you knew.
I hurried as fast as I could.

I didn't want to keep Jayden and Nick waiting.
I didn't want to keep you waiting.

When I came out
to wash my hands, you were
fixing your hair.
"Hey," I said,
trying to look as upbeat
as you so obviously felt.
"Let's go," you said,
talking to me but
looking at yourself.

How many minutes
were we in there?
Four?
Six?
Enough to change
everything.

We stepped
from the bathroom to find
two cardboard aliens,
one of them wearing
a black fedora.

Shame

Shame is
like being caught
naked
under fluorescent
lighting. Nothing
hidden. Not a pimple,
a goose bump,
a hair follicle.

Her eyes sparkled,
her jaw slack,
her mouth hung open though
no air moved in or out.
And then the shame,
rolling in like a tidal wave,
shoving itself against
her forehead,
her cheeks,
those sparkling eyes, until
her face and neck
bulged with it.

In the very moment when she'd
opened up her smile, her arms,
her heart, her beautiful self,
she'd been slapped down, and I
watched her
under those fluorescent lights,
rearranging before my eyes.

She loathed me
for seeing it.
Loathed me
for knowing
that she loathed herself even more
for feeling it.

"You took for-
fucking-ever, Eve."

"Lid?"

"You sat your twisted
ass in that stall
all fucking day
because you couldn't
stand to see it work out for me.
You just
couldn't

fucking
stand it."

I watched her
struggling under the weight of
every single moment in her life
when she'd felt
different and
awkward and
ugly and
deformed and
wrong,
just fucking wrong.
Yet I couldn't stop
myself.

Twisted.

I couldn't.

Twisted.

...And I didn't.

"The hand came
yesterday."

She froze as my words
made their way
through her body,
searching—I guess—for
some spot where they made sense. But
none of this made sense, so she turned and
walked away.

"Lidia!" I called.

She didn't
answer. Then, or
ever.

Lidia Banks Never Needed Two Hands

SHE HAS MY BACKPACK.

"Your boyfriend dropped this at PD. I guess he didn't realize you'd be too chickenshit to show up."

Her first words to me in exactly two months. All those Roxy moments...imagined. But I knew this. I always knew.

"That class was your idea," I say, not taking my eyes off my backpack. *"Everything* was always your idea."

I know the comment will piss her off...but my brain is spinning, my body is spinning. And I have no control. I can't look at her. I can't see her. All I see is my Roxy.

I snatch for the bag.

She takes an easy step back. Out of my reach. Physically graceful, as always. Unlike me. Even now. *Fixed.* Ha. I am so far from fixed...especially because I don't even know what was broken. Just that something was. And it was never my spine.

She is looking at me now. Really looking at me. "What is wrong with you?" she asks, seething with disgust.

"Give me my fucking backpack."

"Why did you do it?" she accuses.

The box. Her hand. I shut down. Totally shut down.

"Tell me!" she demands.

I stumble backward, my thighs hitting the cot. "I don't know. I don't know."

Her mouth writhes in anger and she stares daggers through me. I feel them, every single one of them. And I deserve them. I deserve them.

"Lid...I didn't know. He'd...they'd...you know." The sound of my voice seems only to feed her anger. "I thought we would stay home. If it didn't come. You know. We wouldn't go. And it would be like always."

"That was my hand!"

"I know."

"*My* fucking hand!"

I drop my head. "I know."

I want her to hate me like this. I want it to hurt. Hurt like someone is severing me in half.

"Lidia." It's all I can say. So I say it again and again. "Lidia. Lidia. Lidia."

"God, Eve," she snaps, whipping my backpack onto the cot and turning toward the door. She is leaving. Again.

"I should have texted you when it came," I shout.

She stops.

"No, I should have called you ... screaming at the top of my lungs that it had arrived. It was here. And then I should have met you at the curb out front holding the box. Ready to be there for you, for anything that happened next."

She turns around. Her eyes stare into mine. "Why didn't you?"

"You know why."

"Why."

"Lid—Lid," I stammer.

"Why!" she demands.

"You didn't need two hands," I whisper.

She takes a step toward me, throbbing with so much anger that her voice is thick and heavy. "Who the fuck are you to tell me what I need."

"I know, I know that, Lid. I was wrong."

"You know what I know, Eve? They can shove a thousand steel rods up your ass and you'll still be a spineless piece of shit."

I step back in shock ... not at her words, but by how long I feel she has been waiting to say them. And worse, knowing what she wanted to hear.

"Oh, I have a spine," I spit. "A straight one, now."

We are tearing our world into little pieces. Tiny, tiny pieces. Pieces we both know we'll never be able to glue back together.

"Too bad you'll always be twisted on the inside, Eve," she says, turning and leaving.

This time, I let her go.

Ms. Kisner breezes into the office. "Well, Ms. Banks was sure in a hurry," she says.

"I don't feel well. I'm going to call paratransit."

"Okay, missy," she says. "Let me do it."

I let her do it.

Food Fight

MY PHONE IS RINGING. THE WORLD IS DARK. THE HOUSE IS quiet. I have no idea what time it is.

It's Mary Fay. And it's six.

I don't pick up. Instead, I slide back into the silence, protected by the thickly collaged walls of my bedroom.

It rings again.

Again, it's Mary Fay. And I see it's the fourth time she's called me. She leaves a message. I'm sure it's something about food. It's always about food. Before I can slip away again, I hear the front door close with a thud.

"Hello!"

It's Thomas.

I pull the covers tighter around me. If I just keep quiet, he'll leave.

"Eve?"

I can hear him clomping through the house. I pull the

covers all the way up over my ears and smoosh my face into my pillow to become one with my bed. While

three Roxy
pulsate,
pulsate,
pulsate through my body.

"I know you're here," he calls. "Since you left the front door wide open."

Oh, for god's fucking sake. Did I have to fall in love with the most annoying person ever?

Love? Shit.

"Mary Fay called me." He's basically shouting now. "She asked me to pick up a pizza. Because she won't be home until late."

Does he remember that he kissed me under the portico? Did he kiss me under the portico? Or did I dream it? I hope I'm dreaming this.

"I have pizza, Eve!"

I whip back my covers, wipe the drool from my mouth, and Nancy myself out of bed.

———

A pizza sits on the dining room table...next to a stack of homework. Great. It's not a dream, it's a nightmare.

Thomas walks out of the kitchen holding plates and napkins. The sight of him erases my anger. Mostly because...

god, he's cute, and I think this even though I know I should be thinking, *god, he's kind,* because he is setting the dining room table for two. Napkins, plates. Both Mary Fay and Thomas are better at parenting than my own mother. Strangely, this makes me miss her even more.

The smell of pizza is strong. My stomach growls. Maybe I am hungry?

"So," he says, setting down the plates. "School killing your vibe, Eve?"

He's exactly the Thomas I know so well. And I roll my eyes while I stumble into the seat across the table from him.

He starts eating. Or inhaling. I watch him finish off his first slice and reach for a second. At least Mary Fay won't be suspicious about me not eating tonight when she comes home to an empty pizza box.

Noticing I don't have any pizza on my plate, he plucks a slice from the box and plops it in front of me. He returns to eating but doesn't take his eyes off me.

"Nice hair," he says.

I can feel it standing on end. . . . In fact, I can see it tangling about in the corners of my eyes. And I'm still in my skinny jeans because I'm trapped in them until someone else peels them off me. Otherwise, I'm only in my brace and body sock. I know I look like shit. I certainly feel like shit.

He stops eating. "Eve, why did you walk away today?"

My heart stings. I guess he did kiss me under the portico. Although instead of remembering his kiss, I remember her eyes.

"I had to get to class."

"Well," he says, "I guess we both know that is some genuine bullshit."

"You don't know anything," I snap. Because...I don't know why. Because he's right? But why does this make me angry? And I am angry. Really angry.

He sucks in his lips against his teeth. "Seriously, Eve. I'm just worried about you. And since we're"—he hesitates, but then finishes—"friends..."

"We're not friends. I don't have any friends."

"Eve—"

I cut him off. "Stop saying my name."

He looks right into my eyes. And I see he sees it. Everything that's wrong. That's been wrong.

"Eve."

I hate the way he says my name. I shove my plate across the table. "Get out," I snap.

"You aren't eating."

"I said, get out."

"And you seem to be on a lot of drugs for someone so far out from surgery."

"What are you, a fucking doctor now?"

My face is burning. My chest is burning. My entire being is burning. And I want it to. All of it. To burn, burn, burn.

"Eve."

Now I just might kill him.

"GET OUT."

He starts to clean up our plates and napkins.

"I said, GET THE FUCK OUT!"

He sighs and puts everything down. Picking up his car keys, he heads to the door.

"And don't pick me up in the morning," I say, sounding like I'm five years old, "because I'm not going to school."

He opens the door, and then turns back. "I'll be out front at 7:10 a.m., Eve."

I meet his exasperating compassion with fury, picking up his half-eaten piece of pizza and whipping it at the closing door. But I'm so weak, *and drugged*, that it flies about five feet and hits the rug.

Still furious, I pick up my slice and throw it, too.

It doesn't even make it five feet.

———

And then I eat my dinner.
It's small and
white and
tastes like
shit.

My Decision

The front door opens.
Mary Fay.
I can tell by the heavy key chain and
light step.
She heads for the kitchen.

I cleaned my pizza fit,
leaving the last four slices
on the counter.

I hear cardboard slide against
cardboard, and then her
happy exclamation at the little
amount left over.

It depresses me even
further.
Her joy over
nothing.

Two seconds later,
the floor creaks outside my door.

I shut my eyes. My heart,
pounding.

"Hey, Eve?"
"You up?"

I lie stiffly,
aching to respond. To
tell her I love that she made me
homemade fish sticks and
toast to go.
That I'd talk. If I could.
But I can't.
Because that would mean
surrendering
all one hundred and
forty-four
halves.

The creaks
head off into
silence.
I fill it
with the deep sobs
I've been holding back
since I heard her car
pull up and turn off.

"Shhh," he says.
"Thomas?" My heart
flutters to life.

"Eve."

He says my name like
he owns me. Maybe
he does.

"The pact." I sigh, sinking
back onto the bed, suddenly
so tired. "You asked if I cared
about Minnesota."

"You said you didn't, Eve."

His voice is inside my head now.
It's a part of me.

I feel for the single baggie,
all of my beautiful,
beautiful Roxy
gathered together.
Everything I want.

"I don't make the rules, Eve," he says.
"You make the rules."

Yes.
I decide.

Clutching my Roxy,
I roll sloppily from bed,
slide to my knees, and
drag it out.
The box.
Her box.

I pull it onto my lap.

It's never been opened.
I never thought I'd open it.
I don't want to open it.

I do.

There it is.
Nestled in clear plastic
air pillows.
Lidia's hand.

The truth is
I didn't want her to have it.
The truth is
I wanted her to be happy
the way she was,

in case I needed to be happy
the way I was.
The truth is
I was happy the
way I was.
So was she.
The truth is
I also wasn't.
Neither was she.

I reach for it,
afraid to touch it.
She was afraid, too,
reaching out on that long-ago red rover day,
waiting for the hand to arrive,
dressing for the date.
She was afraid, too.
All this, I knew. All this I'd
always known.

I take her hand.
It feels...not at
all like Lidia.

"It's fake," he whispers from deep inside me.
"Just like your friendship."

I look around my room
at my life—tacked,
taped, and glued onto
the green walls.

"No," I tell him.
"You're wrong."

Me and Lidia.
Me and Lidia. Me and Lidia.
MeandLidiaMeandLidiaM
eandLi
dia.

The truth is
we had become bad
for each
other. For now.
For today.
Maybe not tomorrow.
But today.

I look down
at an arm
that ends in a hand-
ful of Roxy.
My hand.
I place it

all
in her hand
and close the lid.

"Eve."
This time it's my own voice
I hear in the dark.
"Hold on."

And I do.

Author's Note

Fix is not a memoir, but it is the most autobiographical novel I've ever written. Like Eve, I was born with large, progressive thoracic/lumbar scoliosis. Like Lidia, one of my close childhood friends was born with congenital amputation of the hand. Neither plot nor personality is pulled from our lives, but many of our feelings splatter these pages.

As a child, I was taught to accept, respect, and love myself. Simple ideas that become much harder for folks with disabilities, as hate, disrespect, and nonacceptance are often built into the laws, policies, and social and cultural norms around us. This institutionalized discrimination is so strong that it permeates hearts and minds, including the hearts and minds of disabled people—we call this internalized ableism.

It has been well documented that internalized ableism can be associated with negative health outcomes, achievement gaps, and, of course, poor self-esteem. This internalized oppression is further complicated by race, gender, sexuality, class, and age. As a teen, I found it nearly impossible to separate how society saw me from how I saw myself. I still struggle with this as an adult.

Also, like Eve, acute and chronic pain have been a part of my life. Relieving pain is complex and often includes pain medication (such as opioids), which can be addictive. Balancing pain and the risks presented by opioids is a constant battle. Sadly, part of this battle is dealing with the social disapproval of substance dependence. There are, however, people out there who not only understand but can help.

Resources for Information on
Addiction and Chronic Pain

NIDA (National Institute on Drug Abuse)—
https://www.drugabuse.gov/

NIDA for Teens—https://teens.drugabuse.gov/

SAMHSA (Substance Abuse and Mental Health Services
Administration)—https://www.samhsa.gov/

NIH (National Institutes of Health)—
https://www.nih.gov/

AHRQ (Agency for Healthcare Research and Quality)—
https://www.ahrq.gov/

Living disabled can be challenging, but it's one of my favorite parts of being me. It has helped to form who I am and how I move through the world.

Acknowledgments

Among the avalanche of advice my great-grandmother Rachel Benson gave me was that all thank-you notes should be written in cursive. I've been attempting to follow her advice all my life, even if a bunch of it has gotten me in some pretty hot water over the years. My nana was a self-proclaimed pot stirrer, but she was also one of the smartest and kindest people ever. Lucky for me, I am a magnet for smart, kind people. Without the help and advice of these wonderful folks, _Fix_ would not exist. Eve, Lidia, and I owe you all our sincere thanks!

Patricia Alvarado
Sarah Cassell
Leslie Caulfield
Jennifer Salvato Doktorski
Marisa Finkelstein
Karina Granda
Alexandra Hightower
Maria Hykin
Amanda Jenkins

Adrienne Kisner
Alaina Lavoie
Cara Liebowitz
Luz Maldonado
M. K. Murphy
Christie Michel
Hannah Milton
Kerry Sparks
Victoria Stapleton
Chandra Wohleber
Lisa Yoskowitz

Mark Wylie

J. ALBERT MANN is the author of *Scar: A Revolutionary War Tale*, *What Every Girl Should Know*, *The Degenerates*, and *Fix*, among other novels. She has an MFA in Writing for Children and Young Adults from Vermont College of Fine Arts. She invites you to visit her online at jalbertmann.com.